A HAWK IN SILVER

She threw down the brush and scrabbled at the sheet, frantically shaking it. She found a crumpled handkerchief and, in one fold, the hawk-coin.

Thank the Lord for that! I do have the craziest dreams. For a minute I thought...she stared at the coin, suddenly intent; then picked it up and gingerly rubbed her thumb over it. The pattern of the hawk in mid-flight was gone.

This I don't believe. Hell, no. Somebody'd better see this an' prove I'm not cracking up...I'll go over to Chris.

A HAWK IN SILVER

Mary Gentle

Beaver Books

A Beaver Book
Published by Arrow Books Limited
62-5 Chandos Place, London WC2N 4NW

An imprint of Century Hutchinson Limited

London Melbourne Sydney Auckland
Johannesburg and agencies throughout
the world

First pubilshed by Victor Gollancz 1977
Beaver edition 1988

Printed and bound in Great Britain by
Anchor Brendon Limited, Tiptree, Essex

ISBN 0 09 955480 1

For my mother, Amy Mary

Contents

1

The Hawk

Silver glinted.

Stopping to look in the art shop window, Holly saw the glitter down among the cigarette ends, sweet wrappers and dust. Automatically she covered it with her foot, glanced round, then picked it up.

Silver, cold to the touch.

In her dirty palm in the June morning sun lay a disc the size of a ten p. piece. It was bright and untarnished with a hole drilled near the edge as if it should hang on a chain. On it gleamed the image of a hawk stooping in mid-air to take its prey.

Foreign coin? Special issue? She flipped it over. On the obverse was a woman's head in profile, feral-faced, with long sea-waving hair. Holly thought of the canvas and oil-paints and racks of brushes in the shop. Damn! She thought. Just when I could've done with some cash. Wonder if it's valuable. . . ?

She slipped the medallion in her pocket, her attention returning to the shop window.

She froze. The street was clearly reflected. On the opposite pavement, a man was staring fixedly at her. Tall, dressed in an old shabby coat a size too large for him and with a woollen hat pulled down almost to his eyes. She took him for one of the tramps and derelicts who slept out in the East Hill caves during the summer. Except there was something wrong about him . . .

She swung round to face him but he was quicker and vanished into the crowd of Saturday morning shoppers. Holly glared up the road, at the parked cars and the bright street. He was gone. She paused, shrugged, then carried on walking, fists deep in denim pockets. The coin made a hard edge against her knuckles.

I guess he wanted money. Probably needs it more than me. Too bad . . . Then she frowned. So far as she could tell, seeing only his reflection in a dark window, he had been exceptionally fair-skinned. *And that's what's wrong—he was too clean.*

The heat fried her, making her clothing sticky. Lethargically she sauntered past the little shops of the Old Town: jeweller, junkman's, bookshop, toyshop, cafe and opticians', puzzling over the coin. It did not grow warm to the touch.

Jesus, today's hot! Coming to the end of South Street, she looked undecidedly down the main road to the overcrowded beach. *Not a hope. I gotta get out of here for a bit.*

She threaded her way quickly through the crowds to the Fishmarket. A few minutes later she was at the top of Tackleway Steps, at the foot of the East Hill.

Where it faces the sea this is a sandstone cliff pocked with caves. On the town side a steep gorse and bramble-covered slope has one twisting stairway leading up it. At the summit a grey rock juts out like a ship's prow. Beyond that lies high, wide and grassy downland, the gorse-yellow Fire Hills and Starshell Cove.

Holly flopped full-length on Highrock, her cheek against the warm grey stone, exhausted by the climb. Seagulls and a sudden wind cried overhead. Having caught her breath she lifted her head, resting it on her arms, and stared down from the rock's edge.

Surcombe Old Town lay below, a maze of narrow streets. Houses with ancient red-tiled roofs, white-plastered walls and black beams, were interspersed with shops, pubs and churches. There were miniature cars, doll-people, and sudden inky shadows that resolved themselves into black cats sleeping on dusty pavements. The main road, scaled with cars, glittered and fumed like a summer dragon. She saw grey stone spires and—raising her eyes—the West Hill and the Castle bulking opposite.

Down on the beach were fishing-boats, drawn up on the shingle in the shadow of the tarry-black net-drying sheds. Her eyes were drawn by the line of the coast past the West Hill, behind which modern Surcombe and her own home lay hidden, along to the Marina where the town ended. From Hallows Hill to Gallows Hill a heat-haze hid the marshes; beyond that lay the small town of Combe Marish and a long sweep of land that finished a score of miles away at Deepdean, where Chalkspit jutted out into the Channel. And all the time, on her left, the sea lay flat and innocent and unbearably bright. With seagulls flying above and below her, she seemed suspended in the middle air, out of the sweltering town forever. The silence came down like a wave.

"Hello."

The voice came from behind her. She started awake, disorientated for a second. Then, rubbing drowsiness out of sun-heavy eyes, she sat up and swung round, brushing rock-dust from her T-shirt.

"My name's Fletcher."

He stood easy and unembarrassed, a tall and long-boned youth. He looked maybe a year older than her, and a hand's breadth taller. He was suntanned an even dark gold, and wore denim jeans hacked off to shorts, no shirt, and bare feet. Thick semi-curly dark hair framed a square face, blunt nose, wide smiling mouth with uneven white teeth, and deepset dark blue eyes. She thought, Student? On holiday?

"What d'you want?"

"I saw you down there—" he jerked a thumb in the town's direction "—you found a coin. About this big; silver. Yes?"

She hedged. "Maybe. I found a coin, but is it the one you lost?"

"Mine has a hawk on one side, and a woman's head on the other."

"Yeah, that's it. Hang about." She pulled out a handful of loose change and began sorting through it. "I thought it was maybe foreign. Where'd it come from?"

"Junkshop. Before that—" he shrugged.

Far below, a church clock struck once. Holly absently checked her watch, stared in dismay, then scrambled up.

"Jesus, that's torn it; half-one. I was meant to be home for dinner at one. Hey, catch!"

She flicked the silver disc in his direction, slid feet-first off the side of the rock and landed heavily on the path below. She regretted leaving. Even if he wasn't good-looking, the boy had an interesting face—and it's not so often, she thought, that I get a fella to myself.

"What's your name?" He stood on Highrock's brink. She squinted up, shadowing her eyes with her hand.

"Holly." Then, in case he misheard: "Holly Anderson. Bye!"

She ran down the steps, yellow dust skidding up under her feet, hair flying into her eyes. There was a one thirty-five bus from the Fishmarket, she thought . . .

Fletcher stood and watched until the town swallowed her. He stretched like an idle cat in the sun. Then he picked up the coin from the rock. And frowned. Alarmed, he sought the girl again, but she was gone.

"Hello, Mum?"

The phone box was like a small oven. Holly gazed unseeingly at the centre of Surcombe, tapping her free hand on the glass.

"Mum—it's Holly. Look, I'm gonna be a bit late for dinner; I missed one bus already—"

"Holly, thank goodness! I've been wondering where you were. Dear, your father and I have got to go over to Combe Marish this afternoon."

"What's up?"

"We've had a phone call from Aunt Elizabeth. Grandad's ill; she wants us to go over there."

Holly thought, The old bastard, not again! "Can I come?"

"I think it's better if you don't, dear, really. I don't like to leave you but we have to start at once—I've made sandwiches for you, and you can manage your own tea, can't you?"

"Mum, I'm *fifteen*." Holly sighed, "Yes, OK, I'll manage. Look, don't worry about me. You just stick close to Dad; it's his father. I'll see you tonight."

"All right, then. Be good, dear. Bye."

Holly replaced the receiver thoughtfully. Outside, the heat engulfed her, beating back from the pavements and high buildings. She wiped a thin film of sweat from her upper lip, sighed and pulled at the neck of her T-shirt. With no reason now to hurry home, she leaned on the railings outside W. H. Smith and watched the traffic. Here the main coast road met the main London road in a swirl of petrol fumes and dust.

If I had tuppence for every time that son of a bitch has been 'sick' I should be a millionaire, she thought bitterly. Why should we run round after him anyway? He's got Aunt Liz. Ah, hell. If I'd known this was going to happen, I'd've stayed for a talk with that lad . . .

"Hey, dopey: wake up!"

"Huh—oh, hi, Chris, how're you doing?" She made room

for the girl at the rail, surprised to see her on a Saturday. They did not see much of each other out of school. Chris was an active member of many athletic and social clubs, hardly seeing the inside of her home except to sleep; while Holly spent hours alone in her room with paints and canvas. At school, however, they were inseparable. The arrangement suited Holly—she sometimes found Chris overpoweringly energetic. "How's the cinema business?"

"Are you kidding? *What* business? I just finished being cashier for the kids' cartoon-show—might just as well not have bothered. With this heatwave they're all on the beach. Goddamn part-time jobs!" She was a tall skinny girl, snub-nosed, with blonde hair bleached white-gold by the sun. Darker tendrils clung to her damp forehead. Pale eyebrows gave her face a deceptive wide-eyed-innocent look. Unlike Holly, she was neatly dressed; white blouse and blue denim skirt. "Whatta life this is ... You staying down here for dinner, aren't you?"

Holly shrugged, used to following Chris's lead, "I guess so."

"OK, let's head for Toni's. Got any money?"

"Yeah, I think." She produced a fistful of coins. "Chuck this lot in with what you got; see what we can afford."

The cafe was a mass of people. Holly sat on one chair and put her feet across another while Chris joined the queue. Their voices wove into the cross-mesh of conversation, across the seated people and the gleaming table-tops.

"How much've we got?"

"Seventy-seven pence. I got news for you—somebody's passed you a dud ten-pence bit." Chris tossed a coin. It fell in a glittering arc and rang on the table. Holly picked it up.

A hawk. A woman's face.

"Hell, I thought I'd got rid of that. I suppose I gave him a ten-pence ... oh, damn!"

"What?"

"Never mind, never mind ... I'll tell you about it when we've eaten."

The coin lay on the table between them. Holly leaned back, having finished her story, and swept the dark hair out of her face. She envied Chris her cropped hairstyle, and sought in her pocket for an elastic band to fasten her own back in a ponytail.

Chris frowned. "Sounds fishy to me. You should've found out where it came from. And him, too. What'd he look like?"

Holly considered. "That photo of Davy Starren on his last LP. Like that, only dark-haired."

"Very nice."

"That's irrelevant. This hawk thing, coin or whatever, it might be valuable. Real silver, even. Reckon I ought to get it back to him."

"How?"

"I don't know how!"

Chris ticked off points on her fingers. "One: you don't properly know his name. Two: you don't know where he lives. Three: you don't really know it's his. Fishy, like I said. If it was me, I'd say 'finders-keepers'."

Holly covered it with her hands as a group of youths pushed past. "Like to. But I give it one last chance, I think. He might still be up on East Hill. Coming?"

"Was going down to the pool, get a bit of practice in for that competition. Still ..." Chris grinned. "Davy Starren, you said? That'd be worth seeing!"

"Is it necessary to trail your filthy shoes all over the house?"

"No, Dad. Sorry, Dad." Holly shut the front door and

slipped her shoes off, deciding she'd better go carefully. Visits to Combe Marish never improved her father's temper.

"Go and give your mother a hand with the tea while I lay the table."

"Yes, Dad."

Holly threw her shoes into the hall cupboard and limped to the kitchen. Her feet were hot and aching. She and Chris had walked across most of the cliff but they had not found the boy.

Seeing Holly, her mother smiled. "Did you have a good time in town, dear? Oh—you haven't eaten your sandwiches."

"Had dinner down the town. Went over the East Hill with Chris. Don' worry, I'll eat 'em now. How was Combe Marish?"

Mrs Anderson turned away and began filling the kettle. "Grandad's gone into hospital. Apparently Elizabeth phoned the doctor; said her father wasn't eating and wouldn't get out of bed; what should she do? The doctor came round and took one look; said get him into hospital. Of course, Elizabeth and your father are very upset."

"So I noticed." She thought, I'm not upset—except: does that mean we'll have to visit him in hospital? Christ! She fetched the cups. "In a right temper, is Dad. What's wrong with the old buzzard, then: why hospital?"

"The doctor said—could I have the milk? Thanks—he said it was just old age; but he'd be too much for Elizabeth to nurse on her own. I feel I ought to offer to have him down here, but with you at school and both of us at work, there'd be no one to look after him."

"The house is too small," Holly said resentfully, knowing whose bedroom would be taken over. "He's got Liz. We don't want him living here!"

"Holly—"

"All right, all right. I won't say any more. Just, don't you worry any more, see?" *Because the bad-tempered old bugger ain't worth it!*

"It's a long business . . . and it's your father I worry about. Still, we're home now. I'll take the tea in."

Holly put the television on, depending on the Saturday evening programmes to keep her mind off her problems. She sat restless, conscious of the hawk-coin in her pocket, as the evening wore away.

Silver liquid moonlight flooded her room. Holly lay taut, listening for the slightest sound. Something had woken her; she didn't know what. No shadow shifted. Into the silence came a rattle and a metallic click. On the floor . . .

Her hand sneaked out from under the sheet to flick on the light-switch. When her eyes refocused she saw a small dark shape on the floor. It was alive. A mouse.

Holly stared.

Between its front paws lay the hawk-coin, bigger than the animal's head. As she watched, it tugged the coin with sharp incisor teeth, jerking it towards the door. A fat beady-eyed grey mouse.

Soundlessly she sat up in bed and slung a pillow at it. Quick as she was, it was quicker, vanishing out of the door with a scrabble of claws. The hawk-coin lay in the middle of the linoleum.

She noted the time: half past three. Sleep fogged her head. Quietly she got up, retrieved coin and pillow and crawled back into bed.

I don't really believe I saw . . . I left it on the bedside table . . . so how . . .? She shivered. Then she tied the coin in a hand-kerchief, tied that round her wrist and huddled under the thin sheet. Dropping asleep, she thought she heard a faint eerie music. It wound in and out of her dreams; but in the morning she made a discovery that drove it completely from her memory.

2

First Blood

Holly stirred and slept again several times before waking, burrowing face-down into the pillow's warmth. Eventually she reached out and switched on the radio for a time-check.

Eight-ten, she realised. Sunday. No one moving . . . Mum and Dad having a lie-in. Good. Lazy day for me. Forget school and homework until tomorrow.

Morning light picked out sheaves of paper heaped on the dressing-table, squashed and bent-backed tubes of paint, a shrouded corner of the easel, and crumpled clothes thrown down on the dusty lino. Irregular splashes of colour leaped out from posters pinned on the walls: gold, viridian and crimson.

She rolled off the bed, heavy-limbed, and climbed slowly into blue denim jeans, the rough material dragging at calves and hips and thighs. Her eyes were gritty. She rubbed sleep away and began brushing her hair back, tying it away from her face in one heavy plait.

You look grotty. Holly watched her reflection in the dressing-table mirror. Mousy hair. And grey eyes—what sort of eyeshadow is supposed to match that? And ears that stick out. And you're too fat. God save us, no wonder you ain't got no boyfriends . . .

That thought brought back all of Saturday. She threw down the brush and scrabbled at the sheet, frantically shaking it. She found a crumpled handkerchief and, in one fold, the hawk-coin.

Thank the Lord for that! I do have the craziest dreams. For a minute I thought ... she stared at the coin, suddenly intent; then picked it up and gingerly rubbed her thumb over it. The pattern of the hawk in mid-flight was gone.

This I don't believe. Hell, no. Somebody'd better see this an' prove I'm not cracking up ... I'll go over to Chris.

Quickly she finished dressing, scribbled a note and propped it up on her pillow, then pussy-footed down into the living-room. Bumble, a hairy mongrel, stirred as she passed but thought better of it.

She padded across the room, alert for any sound, eased up the catch and pulled the back door open. Shutting it carefully behind her, she let out a long relieved breath and ran down the steps into the garden.

Although it was early, the sun was high. Already it was hot; the dew was long off the grass. The scent of roses struck her with cloying sweetness. She pushed past the overgrown garden gate, grass and bindweed dragging damp and sticky at her hands. The path ran along the bottom of the garden, between it and the field below. She ran in cool shadow down the tarmac path that skirted the field and sloped down into Fern Park.

June heat had burned the grass yellow. She came under the pines and paused on the causeway between the two ponds. The ducks were out, and coots and moorhens; and a long line of pompous Chinese geese. They squarked and hissed angrily; but the swans glided mute. Seagulls rocked in the glittering water and ignored her.

She slowed to a walk to appreciate it all but remembered the coin, and ran on up the opposite slope towards Park Road and St Kevins.

Park Road was deserted. Holly stopped again to catch her breath, looking back over the tops of tall pines and flickering green horse-chestnut trees, picking out her own window in Stonegate Street. Westward, the park ended at Birchdale Junction; eastward, it ran on down towards the town centre and the West Hill.

Yesterday was fun, she thought. A little bit mysterious, but fun. This is . . . different.

The houses were old, terraced; built of warm red brick. Blue-grey slates caught the light and shone silver. Chris's house was the last in the road.

Chris herself was just coming out of the gate. She greeted Holly: "Just going up to get a paper. What's got you up so early? I don't generally see you before midday, Sundays."

Holly glanced round the empty street. She was nervous, but impatient. "Chris, that coin I had yesterday; you remember what it looked like?"

"Sure. Some long-haired female, an' a bird—"

"You could see it clearly?"

"Do I look as if I was blind? Of course I could. Look, let's talk on the way up to the newsagent's—"

"No, hang on. Take a look." Holly unrolled the handkerchief. Chris picked the coin up carefully by its edge.

"The pattern's gone—no, not quite. Look, you can just see it faintly, like a Victorian penny." She shook her head in slow amazement. "Hey, but this is crazy; yesterday it looked brand new. You're sure it's the same one?"

"*Sure* I'm sure."

The noise of traffic filtered down from St Kevins main road; the morning beginning to stir. Chris leaned back, kicking her feet against the gate. "Bloody odd," she said. "Question is, what do we do? Tell you what, tomorrow's Monday; and first lesson Monday morning is Chemistry, right? So we go and see old Hawthorne, get him to check it out, right? Maybe it's not silver. Maybe it's some metal that wears away quick. He could tell us."

There's too many people coming in on this. Holly was doubtful. "Dunno. If he asks a lot of questions—"

"He won't—or if he does, doesn't mean we have to tell him what's happening to it; just ask him what it's made of. You *know* what he's like—lose his head if it wasn't screwed on. Holly, c'mon; you telling me we can't put one over on *him*?"

She looked again at the coin resting in Chris's palm. "Yeah, OK. Hawthorne's thick as two short planks. We can't lose anything by trying—"

A squeal of anger rang out in the empty street. A tawny streak shot past Holly—she jerked back and saw Chris stagger and fall, screaming with pain. Raking her legs with bloody claws was a ginger cat. Holly stood rooted by shock.

Chris kicked; the cat was thrown twisting away. It landed foursquare and leaped again. This time Holly could move; she caught it by a hind leg and flung it down as it ripped her arm to the elbow.

"Help me!" She kicked out again but was thrown off-balance. Something buffeted her violently round the head. She could see nothing, but when she covered her head with her arms something struck at them again and again. Panic flowered in her. She ran.

The coin fell with a clear ringing sound, and she bent down in mid-flight to scoop it up. A heavy blow struck between her shoulders. She tripped, fell and rolled.

An oily undercarriage dug into her back and she came up hard against an exhaust pipe. She had rolled under a parked van but she felt more trapped than protected. She heard Chris's shouting mix with an inhuman screech, close to her.

She dared look out and, in the narrow frame between tarmac and metal, saw a large gull stalking up and down in the road, its snake-head cocked sideways. The yellow beak was red and wet and the glistening black eye was fixed expressionlessly on her. The evil cawing chuckle sounded again.

At that same moment Holly saw the cat, belly down, preparing to leap at her. She scrabbled uselessly backwards. I'll run, she thought. I'll never make it. I'll throw this damn coin so far—

She heard a car approach—fast. She ducked to avoid the slipstream, heard a roar and a thundering concussion of air, a solid thump, and a cut off animal squeal.

Holly began to cry. Minutes passed. No one came. The gravel was harsh under her cheek, the smell of oil and sweet petrol sickened her. She cried until the hysteria passed; then pulled herself out from under the van and lurched upright.

The cat lay a yard away, head bent too far back and mouth open, gaping to show all the needle-sharp white teeth. Its fur slicked up in dusty points. She had been watching it fearfully for some minutes before she realised it was dead.

Beyond a few scattered feathers, there was no sign of the gull.

Her hands and arms stung bitterly, and they were wet. When she looked down she saw long shallow gashes that swelled with beads and rivulets of blood.

"Hey—"

Chris was huddled in a tight ball on the pavement. She uncurled slowly. There were long bloody slashes down her legs and blood running from her left cheek. Eyes and throat were unharmed. Her face was white and blank.

Holly stood unspeaking. unsmiling. Her mind felt numb. She unclenched her hand. The coin had been held tight enough to leave a circular imprint on her palm. Chris's eyes focused on it, and her face relaxed. She stood up warily, brushing at her skirt.

"You OK?"

"Yeah. Are you—I mean—"

Chris's hand went up to her cheek. "It's all right. It's all right." She sobbed, then caught herself and wiped her eyes, savagely angry at her own weakness. Blood smeared cheek and hand.

"Christ, it hurts." Holly fumbled for a handkerchief and mopped her streaming arms. "Did you see? They went for the one with the coin. You first; then me. If it hadn't been for that car—"

"Don't be mucking stupid. It was rabies. Or something. I don't want to talk about it. Not now."

"I can't go home like this."

"We'd better get cleaned up."

Holly followed Chris into her house—messier than her own, she always thought, because of Chris's young sister; yet somehow everything was always within reach. Now it was cotton wool, disinfectant, and sticking plaster. They cleaned themselves silently in the kitchen.

If this wasn't Chris's place, if she wasn't watching me, I'd sit down and howl, Holly thought. I wonder; is it the same for her? She looks pretty cool . . .

"I want a hot drink," Chris broke the long silence. "I'll make coffee. If me Mum and Dad come down, let me do the talking. And we've got to think how you're going to get home."

Holly thought of cats and seagulls; and geese on the pond; and dogs and swans and squirrels—all now suspect. She found her hands were shaking.

"Not through the park," she said.

Eventually she walked up the main road to St Kevins and on to Birchdale Junction; then down Stonegate Street. There was no one awake in the house when she crept in. She made another cup of coffee—strong and black—and took it up to her room.

The four walls closed round her, friendly and familiar. She shut the window, then pulled a chair up to her old battered desk. It had been shoved into a corner under the Art Nouveau posters, and her sketch pad lay open on it.

After a moment she laid the coin down. Taking a sharp pencil and sipping gingerly at the hot coffee, she began to sketch the fading patterns. A hawk; and a woman's sea-strange profile . . .

I can wear long sleeves, she thought, the plaster won't show. I'll talk to Chris at school tomorrow. We've got to know why this happened—because it might happen again . . .

Chris did not come to school that Monday.

3

Contact

Holly stood alone by the main school building. It was tall and grim. A row of temporary classrooms—the Huts—were squeezed in between it and the outside wall, close to the small side gate. In front of her a grassy bank fell away to the play-ground, the rhododendron shrubbery and, finally, the main school entrance in Mill Road. Long streets of Victorian houses shuttled back and forth across West Hill; Mill Road School spanned the space between two of these streets and looked out west over Surcombe town centre and the end of Fern Park.

It was the dinner hour and the playground was noisy and full; ball games, rope games and fights were almost indistinguishable from each other. On the grass bank, groups of older girls sat studying or talking. Shadows lay like charcoal round their bodies sprawled on the brown grass, and the noon haze of heat lay heavy on them.

Holly took her eyes from the far-off sparkle of the sea and her mind from dreams of cold clear water. There was a girl whom she must not meet if she wanted to keep out of trouble, especially now Chris was not there to back her up: a girl called Helen Gabriel.

Lousy bitch, she thought venomously, picking her enemy out of the crowds. The side gate opened. She noted it absently, glanced away, then suddenly back. My God. It's that bloody boy. Fletcher!

"Hey, you!" The girl Helen stepped out of her group; tall, raw-boned, with black frizzy hair clustered round a narrow face touched with cosmetics. Holly swore in a whisper. She saw the boy stop and stare calmly. "Hey, nobody tell you this is a girls' school? Whassup? Struck dumb?"

"I am looking for Holly Anderson."

"Kee-rist!"

That is the limit, Holly decided, him asking her, of all people. She'll never let me forget it.

She strode across the grass, elbowed through the group and shepherded the boy back out of the gate. There were giggles and whispers behind her and the black-haired girl's strident voice. Her mouth tightened in anger.

"What the blazes d'you think you were doing? You can't come in straight off like that. What are you playing at?" A few paces away from the gate, she stopped. "All right; never mind, never mind. Now tell me: what's going on?"

"I want the coin; the hawk-coin."

"I haven't got it." Quite true, she added mentally, I gave it to old Hawthorne at break and he's still working on it.

It shook his calm. "Where is it? Do you not know?"

Holly eyed his worried face. It was young, almost immature; she wondered just how old he was. "You tell me *what* the coin is—and I'll tell you where it is."

"Is that fair?"

She avoided his eyes, looking up through the dappled sun and green shadow of the horse-chestnut tree that shaded them. The pavement was littered with fallen buds; spiky green maces. The sandstone wall was warm against her arm. She was thinking of seagulls.

"Will you give it back to me now and ask no more questions? It would be safer. You and your friend would be out of danger."

"How come you know about her? And what d'you mean, out of danger?" She stopped, remembering the only recent danger she'd been in, with Chris. "Are you talking about what happened yesterday morning? You *are*. How do you know about that?"

The sound of the school bell cut between them. Holly saw the school grounds emptying with magical swiftness. She was torn between being late in class and being answered by Fletcher.

"I won't give it back now. Too much has happened, I want to know why. Look, I'll meet you after school tonight. You tell me what this is all about, and I'll hand it over. Promise."

"Where?"

"You be around Birchdale Junction about five—I'll find you." She ran for the Huts, not looking back and slipped into class on the heels of the form-mistress.

She sat down at her desk, and began cramming dog-eared books into her tatty satchel. He knew about Sunday—how? No one there but me an' Chris. Or if he was there, why didn't he help?

She heard the black-haired girl and her clique settling noisily into the back row. That Helen Gabriel, she saw us. There's another excuse for her to pick trouble—as if she needed one. Bloody hell.

"Hey, how's lover-boy?"

"That one's *real* anxious to get it, ain't he?"

The voices were an anonymous chorus, she would not look at them; but she knew Gabriel's voice beyond hope of error.

"We didn't think Anderson had it in her, did we? Cocky little bitch thinks she's too good for boys—we thought. Looks like we was wrong, don't it—hey, you having it off with him, are you?"

Holly had learned the hard way that her only defence was silence.

"I'm talking to you, Anderson. Hey, don't you bloody answer when you're spoken to? Don't you?"

It never stops, she thought. Their voices were pitched loud enough for the form-mistress to hear; but she knew nothing would come of that. Gabriel had a reputation for being uncontrollable.

"Know your trouble, Anderson? You're a bloody nympho!"

"Where's the other one, Holly? Where's Ivy?"

"Chris Ivy's a creeper—she crept off!"

"Maybe she's with your boyfriend, ever think of that?"

"Not her," Gabriel chimed in. "She's les. Don't call them two the Holly and the Ivy for nothing, you know."

"You shut your mouth!" Goaded, Holly broke silence. She did not mind her and Chris's nickname; but she did mind Helen Gabriel using it.

"Hey, that little bitch is scared of us."

"You got it, Hel. Scared."

Holly stared at the sunlit world beyond the dirty glass, and prayed for the afternoon to end.

Holly found Chris at home in front of the television.

"How you doing?"

Chris grunted morosely. "How d'you *think* I'm doing? What with me mother fussing around, and me father creating hell about dangerous pets let loose on the streets . . ."

Holly turned the TV volume up to cover her voice, and sat down. "Listen. That boy showed up at school today—"

"He did *what*?"

"—and he knows something about yesterday. So I said

I'd meet him up at the Junction tonight, to sort it all out.
You coming?"

Chris pulled a fine strand of hair into her mouth and
sucked it reflectively. "Maybe."

There were bandages under her tights, and two parallel
red lines marked her cheek. She fingered them. Then added:
"Hawthorne say anything about the coin?"

"Only that it's exceptionally pure silver. Said it might be
antique."

Chris was pulling on her shoes. "That gets us nowhere
—he thinks that because it looks old, now. If he'd seen it
Saturday . . . He was sure it was silver?"

"He was sure. Told me to take it to the museum. Said it
might be worth something."

"Worth a whole lot of trouble!" Chris snorted. "Hang on.
If I'm going out, I'm putting my slacks on."

She went up the stairs two at a time. Holly, holding her
scratched and aching arms, watched in wonder. But the
silver athletics cups on the sideboard caught her eye, and
she smiled, thinking, She has a reputation to keep up. Tough
girl.

The television occupied her until Chris returned.

At the top of Stonegate Street, looking across the Junction
in the hot June sunshine:

"OK, where is he?"

"Over by the newsagent's. Dark hair and Levis."

"With bare feet. I got him." Chris unconsciously tidied
her hair. "Let's go."

"He's seen us." Holly waved, suddenly aware that her
jeans were shabby and that she was untidy and hot. Fletcher
came quick and lightfooted through the five o'clock crowds.

"Hello, Holly. Chris. Have you the coin?"

Chris glared at Holly. "You tell him about me?"

"Not a word," Holly disclaimed. Then, to the boy: "Are you going to explain? Everything?"

"Yes, but—" he was hidden for a second in the crowd, then pushed his way back to them "—but not here, I think."

Holly tasted the traffic's dust in her mouth. People swept round them: workers going home as the factories changed shifts, holidaymakers going down to the beach. She wished she could go swimming and cool down.

"The park?" she suggested, wanting clear space more than anything else at that moment.

"If you wish."

Stonegate Street and the path beside Holly's house was the quickest way down to the park. As they passed the field a whickering neigh rang out over the hedge.

"What—?" Fletcher shied away.

"It's only Strawberry. I'd've brought an apple if I'd thought." Holly pointed to a low wooden building just visible through the greenery. "That's her stable. She's due to foal pretty soon."

The white mare neighed again, hearing them clatter down the hill.

There were several benches under the pines by the pond. Holly picked an unoccupied one and they sat down, Chris as far from the boy as possible—she obviously didn't trust him.

"Well?" Holly prompted.

"The coin is my father's. He is a collector and dealer in antiquities; that coin is one such." He smiled briefly. "I was taking it to a friend of my father's when I lost it in the Old Town—Holly, I saw you find it; but then I lost you in the crowd. It was pure luck, to find you on Highrock."

Holly's thumbs strayed to rub the sticking-plaster on her hands. Some luck, she thought.

"And Sunday?" Chris put in, single-minded.

"That? I heard of that from a friend of mine who lives near to you. I tell you this, you are lucky nothing worse happened. That coin has a whole history of misfortune—like certain precious gems, ill-luck follows those who possess it. Well, you saw. There was no reason for my losing it, save bad luck."

Chris was sceptical. "Your father don't mind bad luck?"

"He has had little—yet."

Holly, doubtful, said, "Is that luck bad enough to make two harmless animals attack us without provocation?"

"Hardly. It's my guess that the cat and gull were engaged in a scuffle over food, perhaps; and chanced to be scared by you—and in consequence, attack."

Could that—? Holly grabbed for the rational explanation, but her memory denied it. They went for the coin. Both of them. On purpose.

"Why not just come and ask for it back?"

"It took me time to find you. And, you kept it Saturday."

"Accident."

"We were not to know that; there are other collectors who would give much for it. So if I could have it back . . .?"

"Well—sure, I guess." I bet his father's foreign. He sounds like a student himself. And I'm almost sure he's lying—but he might not be—I'd like to believe him—and anyway, what else can I do? She held the coin in her palm. "Here."

Then she stared, not hearing his exclamation. The coin was the size of a sixpence, no bigger. Three heads bent over it—it was shrinking as they watched—pea-sized, pinhead . . . Gone.

Holly rubbed her thumb across her palm. A faint silver

dust sifted into the air. There was nothing left of the hawk-coin she had found in South Street.

Fletcher's hand closed hard on her arm. "It was the same one? You are sure it was the same?"

"Of course!" She twisted violently out of his grip, on her feet in an instant. Abruptly she realised he was bigger than her, older and stronger—but not faster, she thought, on edge to run.

"Wait, please. I must think. There's much in this. More than you know." He swung round, staring away from them, unseeing.

"Let's get lost," she whispered.

Chris stood up beside her. "We can run any time."

"Well . . . yes." She looked out of the shade: crowds of holiday makers and rowdy children, and the blue sky burning overhead . . . reassuring. "If we wait, we might get the truth."

The pines creaked above, the underside of their branches dappled with light reflected in ripples from the water. Her panic subsided. At last the boy turned back to face them.

"This changes all. The reason must be found. I admit I have lied to you; but the truth is not believable. Tamburrand —the cat—was sent to recover the coin from you; and because of the gull he failed, and attacked you. But as for who sent them . . ."

Holly said, "Tell me."

He shook his head. "No. You will have to come with me. He will want to see you, my father Elathan, in his own place."

"Where's that?"

"Do you know the reservoir? I will meet you there in a short while, and take you from there. I should warn you; it will be a shock. Elathan is—not quite like the rest of you. But I shall have to take you to him."

"Hey, man." Chris was cocky, and scared. "You just try and stop us coming. Right, Holly?"

She knew there was no arguing with Chris in that mood. "Right," she said. "You're on."

4

The Gates of Orionë

Clam's Hole is a large muddy reservoir north of Fern Park, and Downdingle the stream that flows into it. The stream comes from Ridgeway, the hills that block the town from the farming country inland, in a steep-sided and wooded ghyll that snakes down through Cornton Estate to the Park; as if the country had thrust an arm into the town, reaching seaward.

Holly sat on the bank at the beginning of Downdingle, trying to ignore the sour smell of the mud. She was attempting to make a daisy-chain and failing because her nails were chewed down to the quick.

The view upstream was hidden by elms and beeches that grew on the steep banks. Twigs scattered on the narrow dirt-track that followed the watercourse. Chris stood on a rock in midstream throwing pebbles into a pool, calm and unconcerned.

Taking his time, isn't he? Holly thought. We won't see him again. Dammit. But maybe it's better that way.

"Maybe he's not coming?" Chris missed her footing, recovered and came ashore carefully.

Birdsong rang in the cathedral arches of trees; rustles in the undergrowth were—what? Only the evening wind. The two girls were solitary in gold sunlight.

Holly was not happy. She had had Do Not Go With

Strangers drummed into her since early childhood, and even though this looked like the one exceptional case, she felt guilty. "I got an idea. Let's go back to St Kevins, get some chips and go home. We could listen to my Starren LP."

"One: the chippie ain't open. Two: I've heard Starren till I'm sick of him. Three: I'm staying to find out what the hell's going on. What's the time?"

"Seven, or thereabouts." A pebble skittered past her head and plopped into the water. "Hey!"

Fletcher grinned at their amazed faces. Girl with gold hair too short to touch her white collar, in blue skirt and plimsolls: Chris. Girl with dark brown hair cascading over a pink T-shirt, in shabby jeans and dirty shoes: Holly. Both astonished. Neither had seen him come; he moved with a wood-animal's quietness. He stepped out on to the path.

"About bloody time, too," Chris muttered. "Now what?"

"Up the Dingle." He turned, not waiting for them. "Shall we go?"

"Yes; but where—?"

"No time to argue. The sooner we're at Orionë, the better."

He began walking upstream. Chris followed without hesitation. Holly saw no way out and so went after her. Fletcher set a fast pace. Even in high summer the path was dank and slippery, so they could not spare attention for talking.

The mile and a half of Downdingle passed in a dream for Holly. The place was as familiar as her own garden; she had been coming there since her infant school days and she knew every step of it. Four sets of stepping stones, a safe wooden bridge, an unsafe wooden bridge, then along by a cool stone wall where hanging ferns brushed her face, the huge grey double-arching bridge that carried the main road over the Dingle. A rickety footbridge led them by that, their feet and breath echoing ... Shafts of sunlight fell down between the high banks and lit the mossy steps of a waterfall she had once climbed ... They crossed the last bridge and found the Dingle closed by a barbed-wire fence. Holly automatically turned right towards the steps leading up to Cornton Estate, but Fletcher lifted a stake and set the barbed-wire aside, motioning them through.

We're caught now. She looked ahead. The valley stretched on, a dusky tunnel where the trees grew over and shut out the light, twisting so she could not see beyond. There's no houses up there. What's he at? Chris, you said we could run, I wish we had. There's too many things not explained.

She went on. There was no path, so they must pick a way over the rocks and mud and shallow basins of water. The stream split into a hundred channels. They rounded the first bend in the valley.

She thought, grimly, Well, that's it. No getting round that. Now we'll see what we're here for.

She craned her head. In front was a solid cliff of rock fifteen feet high, stretching from one high bank to the other. It curved back and from the overhanging lip a thin stream of water plunged clear to the river-bed, bubbling in a deep pool. The rock was damp and blackened with scabby moss.

"Wait."

Fletcher skirted the pool, using a narrow ledge. She saw him lay one brown hand on the wet rock-face and press. In ponderous silence the stone went back, an irregular slab the size of a church door; in the gap was a flame-lit darkness.

Holly saw then that a man had come out to stand by him on the ledge, not four feet away from her. She noticed first that he wore a long blue coat—and that it wasn't a coat but a robe with a heavy silver belt—and then that his clothes were the least peculiar thing about him.

He had blunt features, a short beard and a mane of chestnut-coloured hair that appeared to grow down the back of his neck like a lion's mane. His eyes were a startling gold, and slit-pupilled like a cat's. His ears were delicate, pointed, and covered with fine red down. Holly dropped her eyes from his face and saw his hands. They were large and capable, the nails opaque, white and pointed. She looked up again, at his sadly smiling features. He terrified her.

But, she thought, he's beautiful.

"My God." Chris's voice was flat. Holly saw her go white, then red, the two new scars standing out dark across her cheek. She began to back away.

"Wait. Hear me. There will be no hurt done to you. We need your help." His voice was deep, and blended with the falling water. "The boy was foolhardy to bring you, yet I think he chose rightly. This matter of the coin touches many folk; perhaps you two most of all."

"Who are you?" Holly did not say: *what* are you?

"Elathan, Master Sorcerer; late of Caer Ys and Faerie, and now of Brancaer; a lord of the elukoi by my own right, and answerable to none but the King. I am not human."

"I don't believe it." Chris spoke quickly. "I don't believe *you*."

"That I am Master of the Left Hand Art? That I cannot undertake to prove here, the danger is too great, and we are watched. But that I am not human? Girl, I am elukoi: we are an ancient and an honourable people—and I swear to you, if you enter these caverns of Orionë, no harm shall befall you; and you shall leave whenever you desire."

"Well, why not?" Chris was breathing as hard as if she'd

been running, but she had recovered her self-possession. "We've come this far, we'll see it through now."

To Holly, it took only a second to walk the narrow, slippery ledge, feel the damp rock and the spray and step into the darkness of the caves. She felt Fletcher's hand on her arm as she stumbled and she turned to see the stone snick closed behind her.

It was too sudden. Fear had been growing in her since they passed the fence; now she was light-headed and hollow with it, heart thumping fast. She had no voice to speak, no words to say, and she was shaking.

"I had forgot, you are not familiar with things of this nature ... Fletcher, see if Mathurin is to be found. We shall follow."

She heard Elathan's concern, but still could not speak. The air was cool and the change from sunlight to sudden cold raised the hair on her arms. She stared. Rough iron brackets were bolted into the stone at intervals down the passage, holding flambeaux that smoked and flared and smelled bitter and sent shadows reverberating over the uneven walls.

"Bloody hell." Chris scraped a hand down the rock. "That's real enough."

"Come." He shepherded them both ahead of him, down the sloping tunnel. Holly stumbled, hitting her feet against loose rock; she wanted very much to sit down.

They passed arched doorways cut smooth in the rock but the interiors were hidden by fantastically embroidered curtains. Holly looked down each of the many corridors that intersected with theirs but saw only flame-lit diminishing perspective. She and Chris walked close together, shoulders touching.

Reaching the bottom of a spiral stair, they almost collided with Fletcher and another man.

"The boy bid me here. Well?" A half-amused, half-indifferent voice.

"Mathurin; this is Christine, this is Holly. Children of Earth, this is Mathurin Harper."

He stood with an easy grace, tall and lanky, with a mop of fiery orange-red hair. A coarse grey cotton jerkin and shorts were belted with a heavy-linked gold chain. His bare arms and legs were covered with a fine red fuzz and his bare feet were splay-toed and claw-nailed. He called to mind an alert wild animal.

"They be human." He glanced at them sideways swiftly and then away. His eyes were lynx-yellow and slit-pupilled. The red hair did not cover his pointed ears.

"Yes."

"There is word from the King, permitting this?"

"No."

He moved supple shoulders as if to say: well, it's no concern of mine. Holly saw beady black eyes and realised there was a small animal riding on his shoulder, under his collar.

Elathan sighed. "The coin is gone; dissolved into air; I know not the reason. It may be the answer is in my books, so I must spend immediate time with them. Do you take these to Eilunieth, and answer their questions; I will join you later."

Mathurin acknowledged that with a careless nod, and did not watch him go. He smiled enigmatically. "Humans in Orionë? That is new. Come: follow me."

"Lead on." Chris pretended unconcern; but Holly saw her hands clench into fists, knuckles white.

They came to a tall arched doorway, the curtain embroidered with roses and orchids. Mathurin swept it aside, and they followed him through.

It was a room smaller than her own bedroom; L-shaped;

lit by a score of candles. A fire, too small to be anything but ceremonial, burned in the hearth. It did nothing to disperse the rock's bitter chill.

"So you are humans . . . do you not stand there, but come: be welcome. I am Eilunieth of Orionë."

Holly stepped closer to the meagre heat. She saw that Eilunieth was another of these strange beings; a woman of inhuman and ageless appearance, russet-haired and tall and clad in white. When she caught Eilunieth's golden gaze she felt a strangeness that was only dormant in the harper and the sorcerer; and she knew without doubt that these people were of a race entirely different from hers.

"Sit you down." Her voice was deep and friendly. "Fletcher has told me why you have come. You are brave to come, knowing nought of us . . . We will eat; then answer your questions. Silver! Sandys, is Silverleaf there?"

"She is coming." A boy, black-haired, about Fletcher's age but with the elukoi form. He carried a silver pitcher. "Be welcome, guests."

He put the pitcher down on a low wooden table, and fetched seven silver tumblers from a cupboard. Mathurin pulled up a stool to sit across the fire from Eilunieth. Fletcher seated himself on the grey furs thrown down haphazard before the hearth; after a second's hesitation, Holly and Chris joined him.

Some of the fear in Holly was unfrozen by the fire. While the dark-haired boy poured wine, she studied the room. The walls were smooth grey rock. Two heavy dark wood cabinets flanked the doorway; and above these, not framed, were mirrors reflecting candles in reed-like candlesticks. The opposite wall held the fireplace (another mirror above this) and shelves of plain glazed pottery. She could not see down the other arm of the 'L'—the firelight threw confusing shadows.

The ceiling had been left a rough dome, from which tiny cones of rock hung down. Again, shadows leered and flickered there.

Chris had also been taking inventory. "What *is* this place?"

"The caverns of Orionë, in which is Mirrormere; and I am Keeper of it," Eilunieth answered. "All this was here afore we came, but we made a place in it for some of us. Harper, how am I to tell? There is so much."

Sandys looked up. Holly saw in his eyes that same inhuman serenity and thought, He's never the age he looks—nobody could be, and have eyes like that.

"It were best, tell one of the histories. I'll fetch the harp."

"That were easier, aye." Mathurin's head was turned away from Holly, staring into the fire and for a second she saw him against the flames, haloed with light. "I'll change it from our tongue to your human speech. Do you listen to me and mark well it is not story nor legend but plain truth."

Sandys came back with the harp, and Mathurin took it and settled it lovingly on his knees, as if it were alive, sensitive. It was not more than two feet tall, of shiny red-black wood, shaped somewhat like a curving sail. Holly shifted closer to the fire and sat up, hooking her arms round her knees. She had never seen a harp played before, though she had heard them.

Silence was complete. Mathurin played.

5

The Well of the Silent Harp

A flicker of notes like fire: Mathurin plucking harpstrings, thumb and finger; hands moving in sweeping arcs. Holly, amazed, found her throat tight and tears waiting on the painful sweet music that pierced her.

Then he quieted the strings until they were a low accompaniment to his words.

"On a time long past," he said, "we left Faerie, that great Otherworld kingdom, and journeyed to Earth. We, the elukoi; and our close kin, the morkani; and the Starlord leading us, at our demand. Five of our great Houses of Faerie travelled thus, and the rest the King left under regent in the White City. For we did not know, then, that as the stars and the worlds changed, the way back would be lost to us. And now we are exiles here.

"And we made our first home—but this was in the morning of the world—and builded the city of Caer Ys, in the southern islands. And that was a great city, and proud, and carven beyond the art of mortals. Fair was Ys: but in a day one woman destroyed it utterly. Tanaquil of the House of the Hawk called to her the timeless darkness that dwells cold at the ocean's floor; called up the heart and soul of the hungry sea; called to her Rak-Domnu, Mother of Bitter Waters. Then, for she hated us, Domnu whelmed the islands of Ys.

"She looked for none to escape that ruin. Yet three ships

of the elukoi sailed north out of destruction, and Oberon
of the House of Raven was at their head. To him had come
the Lord of Stars, Fyraire; to guide, to warn and to free his
people. And against the Starlord not Tanaquil, no not Domnu
herself might prevail."

No music from the harp now, only a deep throbbing of
the lower strings, like a bell tolling under the sea.

"Since that time they still war against us; Tanaquil and the
House of the Hawk, and Domnu of Bitter Waters; bound
in one fate by oaths that even the Sea may not break, that
breaks all else. And Tanaquil we call Seahawk, and her
accursed House are morkani, 'born of the sea'. For we are
elukoi, 'beast-friends', who of old were great. But now we are
sundered and in exile from Faerie—for the Lord of Stars has
never come again . . .

"And the White City is out of our reach forever."

The last chords faded. Holly came back from visions of
drowned cities to the candle-lit room, where the elukoi sat, as
still as carven stone, and as remote.

A white shaggy-coated hound with silky ears, one red,
trotted in and went to Fletcher. A tall elukoi girl followed,
carrying a tray of plain glazed platters piled high with fruit.
She set it down before the fire.

Holly caught her eye and smiled, liking her at first sight.
Tall, with a waterfall of shining silver hair and delicately
pointed ears, she had golden eyes in a vixen face. Holly could
not have said just how old she was.

They ate. Holly had picked out an apple, biting into it
with little thought. The flesh was crisp-fibred and burning
sweet—or was it sour?—or something differing from both?
—she could never decide. The taste was outside her experience,
but after the first bite she was greedy for more. For pounds,
for boxes, for whole harvests of these strange fruits.

Chris wiped her mouth with the back of her hand, staining both with juice. She looked suddenly at Mathurin. "How much of all that was true?"

"All."

"Well . . . how long ago, then?"

Eilunieth put in softly: "Long and long. The ice has come and gone since then, and the patterns of the stars in the sky have changed."

"And you still fight? After all that time?"

"Oh, yes, Christine. Still. Now it is Tanaquil's daughter we fight, the Seahawk; and her folk dare not leave the water, which is Domnu's protection."

"But you," Holly said, "why hasn't anybody seen you?"

"We have our hidden places; the caverns of Orionë, and Brancaer, our city. It is many hundred years past that we made our law: to stay within such boundaries and to have no traffic with humans. I think no word of us survives, there."

"But still at war," Mathurin echoed, "even over so small a thing as a coin."

Holly rubbed the plasters on her arms. "It was them from the sea, they sent the gull?"

Eilunieth inclined her head: an inhumanly graceful movement. "When Master Elathan comes, we shall disclose what place the coin came from; also, why it had value. You were attacked direct, they tell me?"

"I'll say—!" Chris launched into a vivid account, and Holly let her talk. She found herself on the twilight edge of the group and stood unnoticed. She walked back into the shadowed end of the room.

I was right—tapestries. All artist, Holly became absorbed. The subject was the fall of the sea-city, Caer Ys. Here were high white towers . . . old sailing-ships, canvas bellying in a storm-wind . . . beast-people fighting . . . the island, and an

immense dark tidal wave dwarfing it . . . a cruel female face—
shocked, Holly recognised it; it was identical with the face
on the coin. Tanaquil Seahawk? And down in this dark
corner . . . not seeing clearly, she reached back for a candle,
then bent down and peered closely.

She drew back as if stung! There were dark silks here,
black and purple and blue; in a coiling pattern that reached
out for her. It might be abstract—or this might be a beak,
and those eyes and those claws or tentacles. Whoever had
woven it had only suggested a form, but it was vile and
loathsome. She felt it pull with a dark and endless strength;
and held back. It was putting pictures in her head: bloated
spider, thick wiry hair, looping slimy tendrils, razor-edged
scales . . .

Eilunieth's hand was warm on her shoulder, calling her
back. Holly turned; saw that Elathan had come in and the
others were round him. She met the woman's tawny gaze.

"You should be careful." A finger traced scars under the
cloth. "You especially, she has touched you. No—there is
little danger, if you keep your mind from her. Go back now."

Elathan hailed Eilunieth.

"I have found no answer yet. There be books I need that
I have not here; but I must find the answer, and quickly.
Lady, is all told?"

"Our history. I am minded also to do this: take them and
show what part that coin played. Is that well, think you?"

A scratching sound came from the corner of the room and
Holly saw a bird perched on the back of Eilunieth's empty
chair. It cawed rustily; dark, glossy and twice the size of a
crow, though similarly ill-omened. A raven. Then it spread
the untidy fans of wings and tail, made a short glide to
Eilunieth's shoulder and cawed again. She answered in a strange
tongue, breathy and liquid.

The elukoi language? Holly thought. Then she said cautiously: "That would explain how you got a cat to attack us, yes?"

"What you think; that is true. I understand her speech, and she knows the meaning of the elukoi tongue; so though it may be we cannot speak each other's language, yet do we understand each other right well. Tarac bids me recall the laws of Oberon—but this is Orionë, not Brancaer; and I am Lady here." She stepped gracefully between them. "I will take you now to Mirrormere. Follow me."

Fletcher and Elathan came with Holly and Chris. The pale wine had warmed Holly; she didn't notice the chill in the passages.

"Can you talk to other animals?" she asked Fletcher curiously. There was a strange mood on her; she was past doubting anything.

He nodded. "There are few we cannot speak to. You should come to Brancaer . . . they live with us. They are not animals. They are . . . people in different shapes." He saw the others had drawn ahead. "Come on; let us get down there."

"Down? How far underground are we?"

"Not far. Most of it is on a level with the lower river-bed but Mirrormere is lower than that."

They went down a narrow stair cut in the rock, into passages narrower and smaller, but still well lit. The air was still and heavy. At a narrow curtained arch Holly hung back, nervous.

"There is no danger. Enter."

They beheld Mirrormere.

This was no carven room but only a rough cave, narrow at the arch but widening ahead. The uneven floor and sheer high walls were blue-grey stone, alternating with sheets of clear rock crystal. Veins of crystal sang and flashed with light

in the high-vaulting roof. Where the cavern widened and
ended was a pool, very deep, nearly a well. The surface was
three yards across, almost circular, save where it met the wall.
Tall tripods of black iron stood around it, supporting fountains of candles. The saffron flames were tall and still, but the
light and the surface of the water were in constant movement.

"It's like being inside a diamond . . ." Holly whispered.
Tinkling sounds echoed in the crystals.

A raised ledge surrounded the pool. Elathan and Eilunieth
were bending over it. The Lady turned, cat-graceful.

"Come see. Here was your coin."

Sunken in the ledge was a single glittering row of coins,
edge to edge, all round the pool. Near Eilunieth one space
was filled by a blank rough new-forged disc.

Holly knelt by the pool, stone rough under her knees, Chris
leaning over her shoulder. The light stained the underside of
their faces with rainbows.

Coins set edge to edge—here a hawk pouncing, a raven
with head cocked sideways, a spray of leaves and berries that
she recognised as rowan, a beast-man's face, Tanaquil, tall
towers and spires . . . the pool's light ran like water in the
silver metal.

They're not the same, she realised, these have got lettering
—or some have, anyway. And mine was better made. Older,
I guess.

The continually ruffled surface of the water shot facets of
light across the cave. Holly couldn't see the bottom of the
pool; only a dark shadow there.

"What does it do?"

"I will show you." Taking up a long-handled snuffer,
Eilunieth set about extinguishing the candles. They died,
sending up thick coils of pungent white smoke. When the
last candle was put out, the cave was not dark. Brilliant white

light spilled out from the pool itself, sparkling like the sun on the sea. Holly breathed in sharply, and let it out in slow wonder.

Behind them in the shadows, Elathan said, "Two things Mirrormere will do. The pool preserves things, so long as they be immersed in it. The other—you will shortly see."

The pool was quietening. Soon it lay smooth as a pane of glass. Holly, peering down, saw what stood on the crystalline floor.

"It's a harp, a proper one—I mean, full-sized."

"There is the Harp of Math, which has lain there since we brought it on the ship *Brandhu* from Ys's ruin. It is one of the three oldest things in the world."

"It's beautiful." The water had a smell, she found, like lemonade or ice or snow; it stung her nose. "Does the water preserve the coins?"

"No. Over them I have placed binding spells."

"The other property of Mirrormere is this." Eilunieth stretched her hand out over the water.

On the still surface images gathered. Houses, hills, trees; seen from above, clear and minute. Cars moving in the streets and people walking, coloured lights along the seafront; the East Hill, Surcombe centre, Birchdale Junction ... Holly gripped the ledge: eagle-winged, falcon-sighted, suspended a mile above the coast.

"Thus we saw you Sunday," Elathan explained. "It is the eye of the Hollow Hills, our surest defence in the war with the sea. They cannot take us unaware. That is why we must dwell here, as well as in Brancaer; so may we guard both places."

Eilunieth's face was sombre. "Here is what I guard. The well of the silent harp, the eyes of the elukoi ..."

Holly looked again at the join in the circuit. "I got a

question. The coin belongs here, but I found it in the Old Town—how come?"

"That," Elathan was grim, "is the heart of the matter. And I do not know."

"Mathurin Harper came to me, discovering that the coin had gone. I made whole the Well, then, using it, searched out the missing coin—" she turned to Holly "—and we sent the boy Fletcher to you, for he may pass as human where we may not. And so we have watched him, even tonight, and his bringing you here, which was needful. For this is unknown, and in the unknown lies danger."

"Suppose somebody took it—?"

"But we do not come among humans. And they may not come to us, save that we wish it . . ." She and Elathan seemed almost fearful. She said, "Children of Earth, you be cold here. Shall we go?"

Holly cast a last look at Mirrormere. As Elathan relit the candles it lost its smoothness and rippled with inner convulsions. Dappled diamond light flickered.

"I'm with you." Chris shivered. "It's nippy down here."

Eilunieth linked arms with the two girls and they began walking up to the higher levels. Holly was conscious of her warm dry palm and the prick of her nails; but something else troubled her. Something about the images in Mirrormere . . .

Elathan said suddenly, "These girls must come with me to Brancaer, and that soon."

Eilunieth eyed him narrowly. "Now hear me—we have broken laws, you and I; for it is not written that the Children of Earth should enter Orionë, or see the ancient mysteries of the Well; and though there is little that they can say that would be believed, least of all should they go to Brancaer."

"Needs must, Lady. For I may not bring out of the city the things I want; that is, grimoires and treatises, star-maps, natal charts, and the like. Therefore must they come into the city, where I may question them, and haply I may find what befell the coin. For look you, what may reach in to us, unknown, and break a coin; that may break more: a cavern, a city—and then where were we? Lost as Ys."

"There may be matter in what you say . . ."

"There is. What befell the coin: that chanced while these girls had it—so it's like they have seen somewhat, even if they recall it not. And that in turn may tell what breached our defences . . ."

Holly interrupted: "Are they of now, those pictures we just saw?"

"Aye, of course; do you think the Well masters time?"

"Christ!" The images had been of Surcombe in the late dusk of a summer evening. "I never realised. My Dad'll kill me. Chris, look at the time!"

The blonde girl snatched a glance at her watch. "We can't possibly get home before eleven. I'll get shot." She looked up at Elathan. "We got to go. And I mean *now*!"

6

Helen Gabriel

The next morning was overcast, grey light flooding in from the east. Holly walked up to Birchdale Junction a long time before the school bus was due—she was glad to be out of the house, away from her mother and father.

All that fuss, she thought wearily, over being an hour late. One lousy hour. What if I was Gabriel and didn't get in till three in the morning; or that slut Cath that stays out all night—what would they do then, if I was like them?

She remembered the shouting and the tears remotely, as if it were not she who had faced her father's stern righteousness and her mother's more-sorrow-than-anger reproach. They had wanted to know where she had been, and why she had not phoned; and there was no way she could tell them. She had been out with Chris—it was her own business —she wasn't a kid any more—they had no right to pry ... and so it had gone on, till past midnight. In the morning she went through the motions of apology but it meant nothing; it had all happened too often, and she no longer cared.

The queue had grown to three dozen by the time the bus arrived, and everyone stampeded on board; a flock of tropical birds in their pastel summer dresses. Holly picked a downstairs seat and flung her satchel on the one by it, waiting until Chris should get on at the next stop.

Worth it, though, she thought, staring out of the window. Already the clouds were splitting apart, riding the wind over the eastern horizon. Despite all the arguments, she had woken with a feeling of unidentified pleasure, as if she had been given a present, or as if it were a special day, like Christmas morning. Then she recalled the hidden caverns and she was content.

She was startled out of her thoughts by Chris thumping down beside her.

"Hell an' blazes, what a morning! You done Smitty's English homework?"

"Who, me?" Holly fished in the split-seamed satchel and fetched out a battered blue exercise book. "Yeah, up to number four. And don't copy exact."

"I know better than that!"

"You ought to—you've had enough practice."

"So who does your maths for you?"

"So who does your geography?"

Chris gave a wry grin and stored the book away. When she looked up she was serious, but with a deep undercurrent of excitement.

"About last night . . . we'll have to go again, you know. We've got to follow this up."

Holly nodded slow agreement. "He said he'd take us to that other place. Bran-something. Brancaer, that was it. I wish he'd said where it was. I wish we could *tell* somebody about all this."

"Not on your life. They'd lock us up."

"Yeah; could be." But Holly was not thinking of that, she was remembering what Elathan had said just before they left Orionë: "I need not tell you to be silent about us. If you speak, you will not be believed; if you seek, we shall not be here. Nor would things go well for you. I do not threaten. I only warn." The whole hill had seemed to press down on her, and the grey passage contract to swallow her, like a mouth, at a gulp, forever. Then Elathan had opened the gates again to cool air and a thumbnail-paring new moon.

"Up to last Sunday," Chris reflected, "I'd've called this impossible. Now I don't know."

"Magic, they said."

"Ah, no. We didn't see anything last night that, given a lot of time and money and maybe a little alien science, anybody else couldn't duplicate. They may have things we don't, but magic ain't one of 'em."

"Maybe," Holly conceded. "But there's the coin. What happened to that? And how did it get where it was, answer me that."

"You know as much as me, and I haven't a clue. Nor's Elathan." She leaned on the rail of the seat in front, not looking at Holly. "You realise—he's scared? Badly?"

"So's Eilunieth." But it seemed wrong to speak of her and fear in the same breath. "They're odd, aren't they? Different, like. I mean, not just in looks . . ."

She was thinking then of Fletcher, who had said "my father Elathan", and Eilunieth saying "he may pass as human". She thought: he *is* human. If he wasn't, I'd know—somehow. He doesn't have the look that they have, as if they really had lived long enough to see constellations change.

"They talk different, too."

Holly shrugged "Ancient and modern—you heard him say they'd stayed away from us for centuries. I guess they speak it how they last heard it."

"Avoiding us?"

"Avoiding the sea-people, more like." Holly couldn't think of the sea now without shuddering. "Though Fletcher did

tell me him and the harper knocked around a bit outside.
Y'know, curious, like. But I like the way they talk. And
then, there's their own language ..." Holly thought on
that and the elukoi's gold-eyed stillness. "If the elukoi are
true—and they are—then so must the others be; the ones
they're fighting."

"The seaborn, yeah. Goddamit, we should've said we'd
go back tonight; find out more."

"He said he'd send Fletcher with a message. Said not
to go to the caverns in case we're watched." Holly had
a sudden picture of gulls in the park, on the beach, overhead in the skies of Surcombe. A perfect way to watch—or
attack.

The bus shuddered to a halt. Chris pulled herself up.
"Oh well, we're here. Let's go. We can carry this on later."

"Sure." Holly saw her fingering the plaster on her cheek
and searching the crowds ahead. "Go easy today. Gabriel's
in a shit of a mood."

"So what else is new?"

Mrs Smith's English lessons were held in a second-storey
room in the main building, looking out over the town.
Holly made for the back corner seat; Chris next to her.

"Hey you—move your arse!" Holly knew without even
looking up: Gabriel. Chris said, "Get knotted!"

"I said move, you. That's my place."

Chris leaned back, staring aggressively at her. "Is it now?
Might one inquire, since when?"

"Since now. Move, you little bleeder, or we'll make
you."

Hell and damnation. Holly eyed the clock. No chance
of old Smithy arriving to bust this up.

Gabriel had planted her fists on Chris's desk and was
leaning over to spit words at her. The other four of her

clique clustered round. Two sisters, within an inch of each other's height, round-faced, one with straggly dark hair, the other with a neat pigtail: Cath and Julie; a slim dark West Indian with black eyes and hair drawn smoothly back: Pramila.

The last girl leaned against the window sill, uncomfortably close to Holly. This was Diane; small and narrow-featured with a sarcastic grin. Up to a year ago she had been one of Holly's best friends.

"C'mon, shift!" With a casual sweep of her arm Helen knocked Chris's satchel flying.

"Why don't you just leave us alone?" Holly tried to sound reasonable instead of scared, but they weren't listening to her.

"That's fine, Gabriel—since you knocked it down you can bloody well pick it up again."

"Leave it," Holly whispered, hunched protectively over her own books. "It won't do any good. It never does."

"What's this, then?" Helen reached out, flipped the plaster on Chris's cheek. "Ain't no good—you gotta hide a lot more of it! What'd you do—let's see—"

Chris slapped her hands away, almost snarling. Cath chuckled, said: "That boy o' hers. Reckon she tried to rape him an' he give her a good one!"

Filth, Holly thought. Filthy dirty bitches.

The gawky black-haired girl snatched up Chris's English exercise book; Chris made a vain grab at it.

"You give that back, Gabriel, or I'll smash you one."

"Listen to *her*!"

"Big talk, big talk."

"You try it, c'mon, you try it!" Gabriel held the book just out of reach. By this time the whole class was watching. "Well if you don't want it—"

Calmly she opened the book and ripped it down the

spine, letting the pieces fall contemptuously to the floor.

"You effin' bitch!" Chris sprang up and hit Helen across the side of her face. The taller girl reached out and grabbed a fistful of blonde hair; they closed and fell struggling between the desks.

"Go it Helen."

"C'mon, Chris! Give it to the bitch!"

Cath kicked at Chris, Holly pulled her off and was punched from behind; the noise rose to a deafening level—

"*What* do you think you are doing?"

Though not a loud voice, it was heard at once and silence fell. The heap of fighters fell apart and regained their feet. Holly half-heartedly dusted herself off.

"Well?"

"She started it!" Helen and Chris said together.

"Go to your seats. At once."

Mrs Smith was a small middle-aged woman with a bony figure, iron-grey hair and horn-rimmed spectacles—and an uncanny knack of terrorising her pupils.

"This is not the first time I have had to stop you fighting in class, Christine Ivy. You can explain why to Mrs Mortimer. You too, Helen. Go at once." Holly held her breath as Mrs Smith looked searchingly in her direction. "The rest of you, sit down. I will not have brawling in my classroom. With the exams beginning next week I expect you to have more sense. Is that clear?"

There was not a sound, not even breathing.

"We will now go over last Friday's homework. Gillian, collect the books, please."

Holly watched as Helen and Chris left the class for the headmistress's study. Chris was smouldering with anger and resentment, but Helen went with an easy step and a sardonic look in her eyes as if she were not afraid.

Damn that bloody Gabriel. Holly sat bent over her desk, paying no attention to the lesson. Damn her, may she rot in hell. Christ how I hate this place, hate hate hate it. Poor Chris . . . it's happened before and it'll happen again, because when we beat hell out of them they don't stop fighting, an' if they beat us, they don't stop then, either. Christ I hate that girl . . .

Her palms were cold, sweaty; the churning in her stomach settled into a hard knot. She asked to be excused and all but ran to the toilets. She hadn't eaten much that day but she vomited it all up; scalding tears running down her face, and a year's hopeless frustration and hate boiling up inside her until she thought she would choke.

"What happened?"

"Nowt much. Old Mortimer give both of us a tellin' off. Stupid cow. Says it's too close to the exams to put us in detention."

"Ah, she's right. Music an' English come next Monday, History Tuesday. Suppose we'll be revising like crazy all weekend."

"Yeah . . . some day I'm going to kill Gabriel."

Holly shrugged. Her stomach had settled. In place of the hate and anger had come hopeless resignation. "So? Look, maybe you beat her up bad enough for hospital, what does that do? Only gets her friends on to us. And she don't give up. It's—what—a year this has been going on?"

"More. Since about March before last, I think."

"Yeah. She ain't gonna give up. Why should she? Nobody does anything."

It was the dinner hour and they'd wandered into the playground, waiting for the second sitting to be called into the dining-hall. As they reached the top of the drive, Chris stopped.

"Let's take a slow saunter down to the gate, shall we?"

"What the hell for?"

Chris shook her head. "Come on—and hurry!"

7

In the Hollow Hills

No one saw them go. Holly ran after Chris, down the drive to the gate and lower road. She had not let herself expect to see Fletcher, because of a superstitious feeling that, if she did, he wouldn't be there. But he was leaning idly against the wall, and nodded recognition.

"What's going on?" Chris demanded.

Holly added, "And when?"

"Should we talk here?" he indicated the school. Only the highest windows were visible over the rhododendron hedge; but still, they could be seen.

"How about the Park?" she suggested.

Chris made a disapproving face. "What about dinner? I'm starved. Hey, what say we go down Toni's? Go up the back way, no one'll notice. I got some cash left from the weekend."

"Did we ought? I mean, you *know* what they're like about leaving school in the dinner-hour. It only wants one of Gabriel's mob to shop us—"

"Hollybush, you worry too much. Come *on*."

The town was crowded. They threaded between the people like needles through tapestry, the traffic's noise in their ears, its dust in their throats. They reached Toni's, bought sandwiches and Coke (which Fletcher refused) and took possession of a corner table.

The boy scratched his tangled hair with a dark hand, sunlight striping his naked shoulders. Holly thought he looked about him as if it were the first time he'd been in a cafe— and realised, shocked, that it might be just that.

Chris ripped her sandwich apart, eating with an animal devotion. She took a quick drink, wiped her mouth, then jabbed a thumb at the boy. "OK. Give. How goes it? Know any more about the coin?"

"As to that, my father knows what happened to it—but not why."

There he goes again, Holly thought. Father. No way. No way! "All right, what did happen to it?"

"It's common with old things out of Ys—coins, brooches, daggers and the like—to put a binding spell on them; so that time does not decay them. In a like way, it touches not Brancaer. Thus do they keep the same ageless, deathless, and unaltered state that was kept in Faerie."

Holly, hearing the change from correct to archaic English, suddenly thought, When he does that, he's thinking in elukoi, and translating it. I bet that's it.

"Now, as to the coin, its binding spell was broken or ended somehow and so it lay bare to time and fell into dust, so old it was."

"And you don't know why?"

"Elathan favours this: it may be something that scientist-tutor of yours had a hand in; our magic and your science was ever an ill mix. For Faerie is the heart of magic, and Earth is far from that centre; so the magic here is weak, and may be overshadowed."

Chris tilted her head back, draining the last drops from her can of Coke. The sun made an aureole of her fair hair. She seemed to Holly suddenly very young and very confident.

"Speed up," she checked her watch, "me and Holly's got to get back to Mill Road, remember? So: what happens now?"

"Elathan wants you in Brancaer itself," Fletcher said. "For questions and also—since there may be no easy answer —for the Council. And that is seven days before the mid-summer solstice; in your time, next Saturday."

Chris shook her head, doggedly puzzled. "I hear Brancaer this-that-and-the-other and Hollow Hills and—what the hell are they?"

"Our dwelling-places we call hollow hills; Orionë because it is in the heart of a hill, and Brancaer—" he paused, then went on "—Brancaer, because it is reached through one. And that city lies in a region I may not easily explain . . . some island or backwater of time, shut off completely from the later years. Come there. I will show you. That is the only way to understand. Would you have believed Orionë if you had not seen it?"

"That's a point," Chris conceded. "OK, you're on. I'll tell me mum and dad we're going out for the day. Holly?"

"Yeah, me too, they'll have cooled down by then." She thought: It's all going too fast for me. "These hills—are they safe?"

"Safe?" He smiled, but it wasn't reassuring, "They are no safer than anywhere else. Do you not know that you live on the knife-edge of danger—all the time? I will meet you on Hallows Hill, four hours after dawn on Saturday. And go there by inland ways. The morkani do not forget."

"But we haven't definitely—" he was getting up, and by the time Holly spoke he'd threaded his way through the tables and out into the free air "—agreed to come," she finished lamely.

Chris snorted, apparently unaffected by the rapid pace and strangeness of the meeting. "What gave you the idea we had a choice? Hey, I hope he don't keep us out too late. There's some good programmes on the Box, Saturday evenings."

Hallows Hill, a green shoulder of the earth with the ruins of a church on it, marks the end of the town to the west. Holly and Chris, about a quarter of a mile from the ruins, were leaning on the parapet of the railway bridge.

The hills retreated inland from the inexorable tide of the marshes. A slope of large-headed daisies fell away in front of them to flat fields split by irrigation ditches, waving tall grasses and stunted thorn trees growing sideways away from the wind. There the dark reed-beds began, stretching to Gallows Hill and Combe Marish; great squashy tussocks that would not bear a man's weight, wide pools stagnant in the sun, and bottomless mud.

Holly turned inland, tracing the twin silver railway lines northward out of sight. In the distance, beyond the steep-faced bluff of Gallows Hill, morning light was reflected from the urban windows of Combe Marish. It was clear enough to see the ancient Downs green on the skyline, the shadows of clouds gliding over them, and to pick out individual buildings of Deepdean at their feet. The white line of Chalkspit glimmered in a wrinkled blue sea. Dark currents snaked up from the west.

They had come inland as Fletcher had suggested.

"What's the time?"

"Nine." Holly stretched her arms, feeling sun and wind. The gull's scratches were neat scabs now. She hadn't slept the last four nights or paid any attention to school in the day. Common sense told her to be glad she was safely out of Orionë, and to stay away from the elukoi in the future. But Mirrormere and the cavern, Eilunieth and Elathan and the

lithe beast-people, all these resounded in her mind like Mathurin's harp-song.

The strange certainty came to her that she had heard his
music before. It was impossible, but she could not dispel
the feeling.

Towering cumulus clouds drifted eastward. Seaward the
gulls mewed, the wind drummed in her ears, there was the
heavy drone of bees in pollen. The red brick parapet was
warm under her hands. And then all in a second it had begun:
Fletcher appeared in the field below, she swung the duffle-bag
with the packed lunch in it on to her shoulder and she was
wading through calf-deep daisies to meet him.

"Where to?" Chris was aggressively nervous.

"Follow me."

They went along the embankment, north, then west,
skirting the marsh. In single file, Holly last, they moved
quickly, hearing the humming of the rails and feeling the sun
burning on their backs. Then the boy turned away from dry
land, leading them to the very edge of the marsh. Holly
wrinkled her nose at the rank smell.

"Tread where I do." He was staring out across the marsh,
taking his bearings from trees and other landmarks that he
knew. "There is one path only, and it is narrow."

But where to? Holly could see only one possible place;
a low gorse-covered ridge that the mud made into an island,
about a hundred yards out.

Fletcher was already ankle-deep in mud. She shrugged
and followed, shoes sinking inches into sour-smelling dead
reeds, but finding solid footholds.

Must be a sunken path or stepping stones, she thought.
No one would find it, ever. Not even by accident. She heard
Chris swearing behind her and smiled. Oh well. I did warn
her about those fancy shoes. Tough luck, girl.

Step by step they crossed the marshes and the path was neither straight nor short. At last Holly found turf underfoot again, a smooth slope scattered with dead gorse. Bushes blocked the view, a riot of chrome-yellow flowers.

Fletcher glanced round. "Now: blindfolds. And this is for your safety, not our secrecy."

Holly did not say: but there's nowhere to go.

"The gates of Brancaer should not be passed with open eyes . . ."

Holly said suddenly, "How do you get here? The other ones, from the caverns?"

"They go far, those caves. East Hill and West Hill, Ridgeway and Hallows Hill, Gallows Hill and further . . . you know little of what goes on below. We can always come out close enough to Brancaer's gate, under cover of the dark."

The West Hill caves were tourist attractions, the East Hill caves had at least been historic smugglers' haunts. But that the hills were riddled with holes like cheese gave Holly a queer feeling, as if not everything down there might be so friendly as the elukoi.

"Now." He went behind Holly. Soft cloth blotted out her sight; she felt his fingers fumble in her hair, tying the knot, then she was alone. A breeze . . . the smell of mud . . . peppery-sweet gorse . . . seabirds calling. After a minute—in which he must have blindfolded Chris—she felt his hand on her shoulder, pushing her forward.

Mud squelched unpleasantly in her shoes . . . a prickling of gorse . . . her head swam and she lost all balance, felt she was falling though the ground was still solid under her feet . . . she burned with fever . . . she froze, clammy with sweat . . . and now a hand was on her arm, halting her.

"Are you well?"

"I think so—I feel sick."

"So do I." Chris, her voice thick and unsteady. "Get this damn thing off my eyes."

"Hold still."

Holly had time to wonder, with fear and excitement, what she would see; then the blindfold was jerked from her head.

It was a forest.

Vast grey-boled trees rose up about her, heavy and ancient, and on them the leaves of one summer shone. There was no seeing the sky for the thickness of the foliage, but shaft on shaft of light speared down into the twilight, turning the grey bark to silver, the leaves to lime shadows, and the forest floor to flame. A woodish odour of leaf-mould and decay came to Holly, and a feeling of coolness, and the clear hard sound of a woodpecker.

There was little undergrowth and the beech trees grew well apart from each other. The ground rose and fell gently, with deceptive dips and hollows full of fallen leaves. She noticed they stood on a faintly-marked track that wound out of sight ahead.

"Pardon a silly question, but how in hell did we get here?" Chris turned full circle and saw nothing but beechwood. "Come to that, where are we? I thought this Brancaer of yours was a city?"

"It is." He pointed up the path. "The road goes from the gates of the Hills here, to the gate of the city."

"Gates of the Hills?"

He pointed behind them, to where two thick-branched trees had grown into each other, forming an arch.

"Oh. OK, if you say so, friend."

"This is real," Holly said. A beam of sunlight dazzled her, gilding her momentarily in the others' eyes. "But where is it?"

"A better question would be 'when'?" He looked over

his shoulder, impatient and (Holly thought) nervous. "Time was, the forest guards kept this road safe. Little befalls by daylight, but we should not stay."

Holly slipped off her plimsolls, rubbing her pale but dirty feet in the thick leaves. Tying the laces together, she hung the shoes from her duffle-bag. They began walking up the path.

"You see it too?" Chris beside her, a muddy sandal in each hand. "If it was just me, I'd reckon I was crazy."

"I see it. It's too real. I suppose we can get back."

"Bit late to worry now."

The twilight was deeper here where the trees were thicker. Fletcher stopped them at the top of a slope, looking down into a jewel-bright clearing.

An elukoi girl half-crouched in sunlight, staring off into the woods as if listening. She wore a short green tunic and a belt with a knife thrust through it and carried a long thin-shafted ash spear. White hair fell unbound over her shoulders, swinging in a bright curtain to hide her face.

It's that girl Silverleaf, Holly realised.

The girl's head came up, unerringly facing them.

"My greetings, brother," Silverleaf said aloud, standing up. "I had thought to see you sooner, but waiting sweetens welcome. And Holly; Christine; be welcome. I will be your escort to the Caer."

The four of them set off on the path, walking in silence through green light and gold. Silver moved a few yards ahead, the ash spear held light and ready, her bare feet treading the dead leaves without sound.

Holly, watching her, thought, Brother? That makes her Elathan's daughter. Yes, there's a resemblance. But Fletcher's sister? Surely not.

The trees thinned to younger growth, brambly underbrush

and festoons of ivy. They came over wide stretches of olive-coloured moss to the margins of the forest.

Silver took her arm. "Look," she said proudly.

It was not the end of the forest, only a clearing a mile or so wide and about four miles long. The trees ended at a great meadow of long grass that dipped down to a curving stream. Through this ran the track, crossing the stream by stepping-stones, and arrowing up to a hill beyond. Past that, Holly glimpsed orchards and cornfields, before the dark line of the forest shut in the horizon. The first shock came. The Downs were gone; and the air was too hot and heavy for this to be anywhere near the coast.

But the shallow tree-crowned hill . . . she saw what Silver pointed at: the last city of the elukoi, the castle of the House of Raven, the home of Oberon, Lord of Faerie—Brancaer itself.

8

Brancaer

For a minute Holly saw nothing but trees on that hill. Then
the sun flashed from a window and at once she made out
walls, towers, roofs, turrets, all in a warm yellow sandstone.
Green foliage intertwined with the stonework, shimmering
in the heat. On the very crown of the hill, clear of the trees, a
high grey tower bore a pennant, motionless in the hot sun.

"Come." Fletcher led them.

Out in the field, the heat struck down. Holly became very
aware, feeling the dry grass pricking her feet, the weight of
her plait between her shoulder-blades and the sweat gathering
on her upper lip and in her eyes. The duffle-bag's cord cut
into her shoulder, the swinging plimsolls knocked softly
together. Crickets buzzed in the long grass; there were flickering shards of colour, pale blue, copper, brown butterflies, and
in the distance music, odd and subtle and familiar.

The river was low, its hot sandy banks quick with bronze
lizards, the stepping-stones dank with weed. Hazelnut bushes
and reed-beds thrived further down. Holly had crossed the
stones before she saw Mathurin lying back against the yellow
earth on the far bank, cradling the small harp in his arms. He
left off playing and watched her until she followed the others
across the pebbles, and then she heard the tune pick up again
behind her.

As she caught hold of thick tufts of grass to pull herself

out of the river channel, the ground gave way and she slid
back to the bottom of the slope, ankle-deep in crumbling
moist soil. Amazed, she found it hot against her bare skin.
She plunged her arms into it, then let it slide away, soft as
flour. Heat, and the sound of bees, and bright wild flowers,
and rich earth that had the smell of pure growth.

Silver reached back to give Holly a hand. They went on,
over the short-cropped turf on the hill.

Holly heard wingbeats overhead. She shrank away as a
dark bird skimmed down, so close the feathers brushed her
shoulder. She flung up a protecting arm, as if attacked again
—and felt it gripped, felt a sudden weight; and there was the
raven on her outstretched arm, glittering black as a starling
in the heat.

For a second she was elukoi, beast-friend, belonging in that
company; then the bird flexed strong wings and launched
itself up in widening spirals and headed for Brancaer.

"Elathan will know we are come," the boy said.

They entered under the trees into welcome shade; into
Brancaer. Holly had little time to look at the dwellings; how
the city grew into the forest and the forest into the city;
Fletcher hurried them on as if he wanted to keep them
unseen.

He failed in that. Holly became aware of eyes in the
green and shadow; of shapes that resolved themselves into
fox and badger and crow, pheasant and hound and fallow
deer, and—with a heart-stopping shock—the grey-furred and
heavy-ruffed form of a wolf. She walked closer to Fletcher.

After a time, as if the beasts had spread the news, the elukoi
began to collect silently round them. Their fiery hair gleamed
in shafts of light. They wore robes of blue and white and
green, with golden chains and silver armlets, pectorals,
diadems, and rings. But what dried Holly's mouth and made

her heart thump was this: all their animal golden eyes were
fixed on her.

She found Chris at her side. Two of the heavy-shouldered
hounds loped up to circle and sniff. She stopped. Chris, fair
hair spiking up in a halo round her sweating face, said nothing;
only her eyes darted restlessly over the elukoi crowd. Holly
flinched from the touch of their cool skins against hers.
Hemmed in, she looked up into a foxy-sharp face framed
with rowan-berry hair. Slit-pupilled eyes widened.

"*Caren aman'th erieu d'chai ara'kayn?*"

Fletcher shouldered ahead. "Yes, they be human. It is the
Master Sorcerer's command."

"*Edu'n, ata?*"

"Yes, at this time, of all times. Stand aside." He added
something sharp in the elukoi tongue.

Holly followed him through the crowd, head down,
hearing raised voices behind her and not looking up until
there was stone underfoot and they had mounted a flight of
steps to a high tower.

"Be welcome." The boy had that odd formality of the
Hills about him again. "This is the house of the Master Sorcerer."

Towards evening, Holly came to sit in the western window
embrasure of that tower. Behind her, Chris and Elathan were
still talking. She had let Chris do most of the explaining. Now
they sat shaking their heads in bewilderment over a succession
of books and strange charts.

Holly gazed round the high-ceilinged room, with its books
and tapestries, the evening sun striking fire from glass retorts
and shelves of stone pots labelled with odd heiroglyphics.
Dust danced in the sun. Then she swivelled round and opened
the thick glass windows, looking out at Brancaer.

Down in the green city the elukoi moved in ones and twos towards the grey tower. Holly watched them and their houses. In every case the ground floor was a stables or mews or kennels or byre and the friends of the beasts lived in the upper rooms; ivy and red creepers clung to the walls and spired in at the windows.

She thought, I wonder how far we really *are* from home? But the idea didn't worry her. She could not have said what she felt: did not know until a long time after that it was complete happiness; that long summer evening casting a yellow haze over the tree-tops, the towers and the fields and forest beyond; and herself up in the window of the tower, eagle-high, catching the last of the cool wind.

"Holly."

"Yes?" She saw Fletcher had come back. The boy was not in denim, for once, but in white tunic and silver belt, with a raven-headed knife in a sheath. She could almost believe him elukoi at that moment.

Elathan stood. "The Council convenes shortly; you must be there. I have bid the boy take you to the Hall of the Three Ships. I will come later, and present you to my Lord Oberon."

They left the tower and headed uphill. The grey tower proved on close inspection to be a main hall and several smaller ones, enclosed by a massive wall. They passed from the city into the shadow of a tunnel-like arch, suddenly cool; and so under that wall and out into the citadel. Framed by the glossy stone, Holly saw emerald lawns, with a gnarled and spreading apple tree in their centre and beyond that the entrance to the Great Hall. Her eyes caressed the lines of rock that time and the sun had worn silky silver-grey, tracing the tall spires lancing dizzily into the deep sky, the towers, the balconies and courtyards, the fountains and statues seen framed through half-moon arches.

"They will not come into the Hall until the King bids them. We will wait inside, that will attract less attention."

Holly nodded. Walking on, she found the lawn soft to her feet. They paused under the fountaining branches of the apple tree and the boy reached up to pull down a ripe apple. Holly watched the dip and sway of the branch, the leaves rustling round her face, finding herself caught in a tent of green light and shadow. He bit into the apple, pulling down another branch so that she and Chris could reach.

Holly said, "What I don't understand is, why they want to leave. I mean I know about the sea-people, but they can't get into Brancaer, can they? Or can they?"

"No, never; yet. But listen, Earth is not Faerie. In Faerie they are the undying, the immortal shining ones—here they are the elukoi, and age tells. It is not the sole reason, but there it is: no elukoi wants to die."

The crisp ruddy apple, rivering with juice, broke white and cool under her teeth. She stared at him for a second, then hastily wiped stray drops of juice off her chin. She thought: Undying? And Elathan said: Oberon. And in Mathurin's song about Ys, Oberon. Is that the same—?

"What happens at this Council?" Chris asked. "It isn't just us, is it?"

"There is the King's decision to be heard, on the matter of the solstices of midwinter and midsummer; the which has more importance now than anything—" he threw down the apple core. "For that, you must ask Mathurin. Come into the Hall. He will be there, I think."

It was not until then, following him, that she thought, *Apples from a tree, in June, ripe?* and looked back. It was an immense tree, old, gnarled, branches spraying up to wide umbrellas of leaves, and in among those leaves were apples ripe as September, apples small, hard and green as June and blossom as white and delicate as April.

On one tree at the same time? But it was there, solid to touch. With a sudden certainty she thought, I'll paint that one day, as it is, and it will be my best.

Ivy forested the walls at the entrance to the Hall, stems as thick as tree-boles. Inside, the Hall was all of light-coloured wood; floor, walls and high heavy-beamed ceiling; benches and tables too. At the far end was a raised platform with four carved chairs. The windows behind it were high and narrow, light slotting in dimly. There were tables where saffron candles stood by the hundred but no elukoi—except one.

It was Mathurin, without his harp, He saw them, smiled and came over.

Holly gazed round, puzzled. "Why do they call this the Hall of Three Ships? I don't see none."

"Three ships came out of Ys; Raven's *Brandhu*, Rowan's *Quicken-Tree*, and the *White Dove* of the House of Diamond. Here they remain. For we came ashore and found the Hills, and took the ships apart to build shelter against that first freezing winter—we were all but in the shadow of the glaciers. And in later years we quarried the stone."

Holly wanted to make sure. "*You* were at Ys?"

"I was. I had a room at the top of a slim tower, wide-windowed and looking out over the sea. In the morning when the air was clear you could see the sun come up blood-red, making a scarlet track over the green waves; the white sea-walls would turn gold and the wind smelt of salt and sea-drift.

"And one time I woke early and went down the winding outer stair and up to the rose gardens atop the sea-wall. And I went down, for it was lowest tide, to the thin margin of shingle and watched the foam go from grey to blinding white and listened to the seamews calling, and saw the curving waves. On that same morning I saw the Unicorn, on the beach, warning us to take ship and avoid the treachery of Rak-Domnu. And it were easier looking full at the sun, than at the Unicorn in daylight. But Caer Ys we never saw again."

"Tell me," Holly said carefully, "about midsummer. And midwinter."

"What of them?"

"That's what I want to know."

She saw the harper look questioningly at Fletcher and then shrug. "Well, they have power, the solstices; longest and shortest days, both. Light and dark. We may use the midsummer power, if we will it. And we fear—we know—the morkani will use midwinter against us; power of cold and dark and death. And we do not know which is right: to war against them to the uttermost—and then many will die—or else, or else . . ."

"What?" Chris asked, when he didn't continue. "What else is there but to fight?"

"This year the stars be right, this year alone and such a conjunction not to come again for uncounted ages. For they be now as they were when we came from Faerie; and so there might be an end to this exile at last, if we could but summon the Starlord to lead us home."

Holly thought: I never realised what homesickness was. But his voice . . . ah, no. Nobody should want anything that badly.

"If we summon him at midsummer with the Harp of Math, that he loved above all, I think the Starlord would come, for he is not bound by Earth or Faerie. And if he comes, there is an end to war and to fighting and to growing old and to death, and there is our way home. It must be

midsummer, if it is to be at all. And the King decides and will
tell us soon. For we be all gathered together for this council;
the House of Raven and such as remain of the Houses of
Rowan and Diamond. Too, there is myself and Master
Elathan and the Lady Eilunieth—"

"Is she here?" Fletcher cut in.

"So; and should she not be? Is this not the one day she
leaves both Flame and Well? Surely she is here."

"I have not seen her. It is not her way to be late."

There was no time to go into it further. Holly, startled,
realised the Hall had been filling up while they talked and
now was crowded with elukoi. They watched her and Chris
with varying expressions: shock, surprise, curiosity, even
fear. She thought, I bet they'd like to get their hands on
Elathan. They don't like us being here at all.

A drum beat twice, heavy and deep, and silence fell. Then
Oberon came into the Hall, Tarac on his shoulder.

The King's hair was white as Silverleaf's. He was tall and
inhumanly thin, brown-skinned and golden-eyed and he
wore a white robe embroidered in silver with signs ancient
and pagan. He passed Holly and Chris without noticing them,
mounted the dais and seated himself in the greatest of the
four carven chairs. One of the flamehead elukoi bore to him
a sword with a bronze hilt and a pommel worked in the form
of a golden apple; he laid the naked sword across his knees
and then she saw his hands. The skin was mottled with darker
brown freckles and the veins stood up as dark blue ridges.
Oberon of Faerie was old.

"Now," whispered Elathan, suddenly and quietly at their
side. "We break the morkani once and for all time."

"I have not heard that. Wait, before you begin your wars."
Mathurin then signed for silence, as the King's deep voice
came to them.

"Children of Faerie, hear me. The solstice comes. I call the Harper, I call the Sorcerer, I call the Lady. I charge these ministers of mine to do my will. Let all be made ready; let the Harp be brought from the Well and at the right and proper time I charge you to summon the Lord of Stars, summon Fyraire to open the gates that are closed, summon the Unicorn to lead us home.

"As I have spoken, so let it be."

Holly heard Mathurin let out a long breath and saw him grip weakly at the table as the tension drained out of him. Elathan, suddenly frowning, went up to speak with the King. And then down by the door was a sudden noise and confusion, the elukoi crowding out and raised voices heard.

"Stay. I'll discover what it is." Fletcher slid into the press of bodies.

"Christine; Holly—"

Holly swung round to see Elathan come down from speaking with Oberon. His face was bloodless.

"What's up?"

"You are to leave—both of you—now."

"Why?" Without reason she felt cold, sick. Fletcher's voice came clear from outside.

"Bring Sandys—quickly!"

"The Healer? Starlord, no! I was afraid of this."

She found Elathan's hand on her shoulder, was abruptly pushed through the crowd and outside the Hall. For a minute she was confused; then she noticed a knot of elukoi bending over something on the grass. As Sandys shouldered in, holding his satchel of herbs, she saw it was a body.

Chris leaned forward. "Christ! It's Eilunieth."

She lay sprawled on her back, arms and legs flung wide. Her skin was sickly white under dirt, her mouth blue and her eyes shut; and all the right side of her body was grazed and bloody. The leg was scabbed and crusted with blood. Holly couldn't take her eyes away.

Another elukoi knelt by her, dirty and utterly weary. As Silverleaf ran to him, he lifted his head.

"I have brought her from Orionë. Well for you and her that I was there. None other could have done it." He spoke haltingly. "The caverns are gone. Fallen in. Rock everywhere. She was sorely hit."

Fletcher pushed nearer. "Is she dead?"

"Nay; but close." Sandys stood up briskly. "Help me move her. I can do nothing here."

Holly swallowed convulsively. As they carried the woman away, her head fell back and her mouth gaped open. Silver helped the other elukoi up and supported him as they followed her.

Elathan said, "You had best go. Now. While you can."

Chris snarled, "I don't know what you're talking about!"

"But I know. I know now what broke the binding spell on the coin. I know that same thing must have broken the guarding spells on Orionë; and so the morkani have brought darkness down full-force on the caverns."

"What?"

"You—" his finger stabbed first at Holly, then at Chris "—and you."

"No!" Holly shouted. "You can't tell us that's our fault. There's no way."

"Human—both of you: human!" He spat it out like an obscenity.

Holly remembered, then. Fletcher had said: the heart of magic is Faerie, and far from here, and may be overwhelmed by things of Earth. And what belongs to Earth more than humans, who never quite believed in magic at all . . .

"We didn't *know*," she said.

"You think that matters? Lord, but I should never have taken you to Orionë. Spells once broken, the sea-people do not sleep. And if all were known, may be they have done worse than kill Eilunieth—" control lost, the anger snarled out "—who knows what you have done to Brancaer already? Get out! Get out before you kill us all!"

9

The Harp of Math

Holly hummed a Davy Starren track absently, dawdling along the top path of Downdingle. It ran through a strip of woodland between the back gardens of the Cornton Estate and the ghyll itself. The stream here was only four or five feet below road level. A hundred yards on, where it dropped twenty feet, she had seen the gates of Orionë open.

She stopped and whistled the dog Bumble out of the undergrowth. His walk was her sole excuse for being there.

So Elathan warned us off—but I reckon all the harm's been done. Eilunieth. Is she dead? Godammit, somebody could've come and told us, that isn't much to ask.

A splintery paling fence blocked her way. Just beyond it a large notice proclaimed DANGER SUBSIDENCE!

Is that what they call it? If they only knew . . . what am I talking about? It must've been subsidence, what else?

"Holly." Fletcher was there among the hornbeam and brambles; somehow she hadn't seen him. "I thought I would see you."

Oh did you? Holly wasn't about to admit that was why she was there. "How's Eilunieth?"

"Living. She is in the house of Sandys the Healer."

"Will she be OK?"

"In time."

Embarrassed, she thought, Is he trying to get rid of me?

He reached over and pulled part of the fence aside. "Go down and look."

"Aren't you coming?" When he didn't move, she looped the dog's lead over the fence and made her way crabwise down the steep slope.

The local paper had headlined it MASSIVE SOIL ERO-SION and made Downdingle stream responsible for under-mining the banks. The small monochrome photograph had not prepared her for the reality.

The ground crumbled away in front of her. Both the high banks had torn away from their foundations and spilled downstream. Four great elm trees lay uprooted down the choked watercourse, branches torn and roots spidering naked to the sky. The gates of Orionë no longer existed; for fifty yards upstream the land had collapsed to the level of the lower river-bed.

Light struck down, glittering silver on the rocks, the mud, the stream. Water collected in murky pools.

What a mess . . . Holly turned and climbed away, feeling sick.

"The fault was not yours." Fletcher held out a hand and pulled her up the last steep bank. Replacing the fence, he added, "Elathan knows that, but he was angered at the Council."

There's an understatement for you. We were thrown out. That led her thoughts back to the Council, and a question that had been troubling her. "Here—what about the Harp? Did it survive?"

"None knows. There are spells on the wreckage that prevent us even going close." He caught her expression of disbelief. "The morkani, having one claw-hold on land, are able to bar us from Orionë, even though they may not themselves come ashore."

"But Mathurin said it had to be *that* harp."

"So; and the King will not go back on his word. The harper must play a common harp, and hope." He eyed her speculatively for a moment. "Listen, tell me what you think of this—the sole way that coin could have got from Mirror-mere to your town, is that one of the elukoi took it. Also this: none knew the spells guarding Orionë had been broken. Yet the morkani knew. How so? Elathan swears there was no sea-magic put on the caverns before their destruction. The morkani were told. And by who? By one or more of us, the elukoi . . ."

Holly shoved her hands in her pockets and stared down towards the wreckage. "That's nasty. I mean, it sounds as if it's true, and if one of your lot is on the other side—and caused this—that's nasty. Does Elathan know?"

"Yes, but he does not believe. True, I half-think he is right, for who could it be?"

"I don't know." Behind them the traffic growled through the Estate. A thrush sang in Downdingle. Briefly Holly thought of falling stones, shuddering earth and pain and chaos in the dark. "That one that brought Eilunieth out—he must've had a hell of a time."

"He came out by the Deepway, that now is fallen in." Fletcher turned back towards the wood. "I do not know what may chance at midsummer, but certainly the morkani will have no time for humans. You and Chris are free of this."

And he was gone.

But—oh, damn! She walked thoughtfully home in the golden evening. Friday, the end of a week of exams, the weekend ahead . . . she was depressed. Tomorrow's midsummer, she thought. And what's going to happen to Fletcher and Mathurin and Silver and the rest? And Brancaer . . .

Leaving the Hills, she had looked back once at Brancaer. It was that hour of the evening when the June sun loses its fierce heat and hammering white light and turns a wine-amber colour in the air. This gold was diffused among the tawny brick houses and the tops of verdant orchards, the grey towers and the distant and strangely-forested horizon. It washed in like a sea over Brancaer and brought Holly's heart aching into her throat.

Later she went over to Chris to discuss things.

"Out of it, are we?" Chris said at the door, when she left. "I'm not so sure. The Harp . . . there's something there I can almost work out. No good tonight. I'll sleep on it. Come round tomorrow morning, OK?"

"OK. About nine. Though I don't know what good you think you'll do."

"Nor do I—yet."

It was one of those hot mornings with an amber haze filming the blue sky, the horizon dirty with low cloud.

"I've got it."

"Really? I hope it ain't catching!"

"Funny ha ha."

Chris slammed the gate behind her and started up Park Road towards St Kevins. "We gonna find Fletcher. I'll explain then."

"Hey—!"

"We haven't got time to go through it twice. From what you said, he's keeping an eye on Orionë for Elathan. We'll try there first. Catch a bus by the church."

"If you say so."

A light wind saved the day from being stifling. Chris was cool in skirt and blouse; Holly was hot in denim, and plaited her hair to keep it out of her face. As ever, most of England seemed to have come to the south coast, but as the bus moved into urban back streets they lost the crowds.

The bus left them at the bridge over the Dingle. They climbed down into the ravine and trotted upstream. At the barbed-wire fence they were met by a barking dog; rough-coated, alert, and white save for one red ear . . . then a voice called "Holdfast!" and the hound was silent.

"Well?" Fletcher at the fence, not looking pleased to see them.

"Very well, thanks." Chris grinned disarmingly. "Hey, can we get to where we were first time, the pool and the gate?"

"I could show you, from here. To go there . . . there have been further rockfalls, there may be more."

Holly heard Chris's indrawn breath when she saw the wreckage; she had decided, in revenge for being mystified, to give Chris no warning.

"Jesus Christ. This is gonna be trickier than I thought."

"*What* is?"

"The sea-people can't come out of the sea, right? And they've used magic to keep you out of here, right?" Chris said 'magic' as if it were a dirty word.

Fletcher's attention was caught. "Yes; and so?"

"This spell-breaking thing works two ways, then. If the elukoi couldn't keep us out then, nor can the sea-people now. Hey, don't you see? Me and Holly can go in there for you and look for the Harp."

"It is perilous. If the rocks settle—"

"Too bad. But it makes up a bit for the other, don't it; if we do this." She hurried on. "Look, we'll go up. You can see us. Shout when we're near where the Well was. OK?"

"There may be a tunnel broke open to the air. Go."

It was slow work picking their way over shifting rocks, under tree trunks, and through deep pools. Holly thought of seaside rocks: the same dank smell and slippery cold, and the fear of being trapped. Once she lifted her eyes and found she was in the centre of destruction. If a collapse came now they'd never get out—then she was bitterly afraid.

At last they rested between two shattered grey rocks, under the crown of a fallen beech. Loose shale glided underfoot. Holly had grazed hands and bruised knees; her jeans were patched with dust. Chris cursed about her ruined skirt, then answered Fletcher's last shout.

"Somewhere here, he reckons. See anything?"

"There's a gap here." Holly kicked with her plimsoll and pebbles skittered down. "Can't see how far it goes."

Chris knelt, then lay down, putting her head under the lip of the rock. "This should do. It's about eighteen inches here, then it widens out. Can squeeze through that. C'mon."

"Yes, but how about light?"

Chris produced a pencil-torch from her pocket, looking smug. "After you?"

"Age before beauty."

She let Chris go, and then lay at the edge of the crack, peering down after her. The sunlight illuminated a shallow slope of rocks. She thought one of them ought to stay on the surface—and then she saw Holdfast was with them, plainly on guard, though he didn't come within the bounds of what had been Orionë.

She rolled in, and slid down the slope on her back. The cold struck her. She was in a narrow, dark and dirty tunnel, and it didn't look anything like Orionë. Chris's torch flashed on beside her and they stood together for a minute, peering up and down the passage.

"Whereabouts are we?"

Chris grunted recognition. "Quite near Mirrormere—I think. That's something. Be careful where you tread."

The pale yellow of the torch was the only light. Holly hated leaving the sun. The chill raised goose pimples on her arms. Now the tunnel curved, and there was an arch . . .

"Here."

She followed Chris in. The crystal was black and lifeless, glinting sullenly where the torch hit it. The high roof had fallen in, blocked again by a massive slab of stone. Holly, with candles and diamond light in her memory, had sudden stinging tears in her eyes.

"It had better be me." Chris stepped forward. The crystal was broken and dark. She shone the beam into the hollow.

10

Changeling

"By God, I was right!"

"Don't sound so surprised." Holly could see the Harp in the circle of yellow torchlight. It lay drunkenly against the dry pool's side. "Jesus, it's big, I'd forgot."

"Help me shift it, then." Chris jumped down, feet scraping and echoing, and laid the torch on the lip of the pool. Polished wood and silver gleamed. "Can't see any damage."

Holly sat on the cold stone and slid into the hollow. The light shone upward, making weird shadows on their faces, and outside the circle the darkness was thick.

The sooner we're out of here the better. "OK—heave!"

They hoisted it, gripped the frame, and lifted it bodily into the cave. Holly, sweating from that brief effort, took the base; Chris took the top and they staggered back into the tunnel. Neither could hold the torch properly. In the half-dark they rounded the corner and came to the bottom of the slope. Holly was blinded by incandescent sunlight, seeing her friend's hair flame golden, the dark Harp glow, and each separate string shine unbearably.

Between them they dragged the Harp up the scree and out of the narrow gap. The sun's warmth soothed Holly's churning stomach. Holdfast whined, some distance away.

Chris snapped the torch off and pocketed it. "Let's get this thing out of here."

"Yeah. And let's make it fast."

But there was no hurrying; no firm footing in that wilderness of stone. Mosquitoes buzzed round them. Holly was itchy and sweating. The Harp was as tall as she was and astonishingly heavy. Heave one end on to a rock . . . crawl over . . . catch it as it came down the other side . . . hold it while Chris got ahead; now push . . . grab it as it slipped! . . . so things went; and the wind dropped and the sun hammered down.

They reached Holdfast. Holly saw his ears were down and his tail curled between his legs. He whined and pawed at them. They rushed the last stretch to the barbed-wire fence, wet to the knees and smeared with mud, panting heavily. Fletcher caught the frame as they half-dropped the Harp. It made a deep indentation in the earth.

"Oh Jesus, I thought it was gonna come down." Holly shook her head ruefully. "All my neck is goose pimples."

There was a hollow grinding bang, and a little dust came drifting round the corner of the valley. The rumbling went on deep down and trailed off in a skitter of pebbles. Holly shut her eyes, dizzy.

Chris raised thoughtful eyebrows. "Remind me to take more notice of your goose pimples, next time . . ."

Then they were laughing and talking all together, all at once; nobody listening, only saying "look what we did!" Fletcher shook his head disbelievingly.

"You did it. You really did it."

"Didn't we just?" Chris slapped the Harp familiarly. "Well, now we got it, what do we do with it? Does Mathurin want it in the Hills?"

"Outside. Brancaer is closed. The Harp must summon in this time. They will use the hill of the gate, in the marsh. Holdfast will fetch Silver, Hawkhunter, Westwind; some others; they will move it."

"You reckon we should tell 'em?" Holly qualified: "Yet, I mean. Look, someone's had one go at the Harp already. If it gets round that we've got it—goodbye, our chances."

A small silence. Fletcher said, "It must be us, then. Hide the Harp, deliver it up at sunset to the hill. Then there is no time to prevent the harper playing."

Chris snapped her fingers. "Got it. The tunnel under the bridge back there. Nobody ever goes there. And we can't take this thing any distance ... Holly, you and me come back about half-eight, and we'll try it on a bus up to Hallows Hill."

"OK." She checked her watch. "Time we was back for dinner anyhow. I've got a dust-sheet in the attic. I'll bring it. We can let on we're delivering this from one of the antique shops."

Fletcher plucked at the strings; they vibrated deeply like bees. He said, "Be careful."

Holly thought she was first back. The bottom of the Dingle was in shadow, but sunlight turned the tree-tops emerald. Evening sounds trickled down from above; a radio, cars, kids playing, a TV. She walked quickly, the rolled dust-sheet under her arm.

The bridge is double-arched. The massive central pillar plunges down into the river-bed. A tunnel slants the stream through it; the path continues by it on a wooden footbridge. The inside of the tunnel is not visible from either up or down stream.

Holly sauntered on to the footbridge, whistling. There was no one in sight. She called softly, "Fletcher?"

"Here."

She stepped back quickly. His head was on a level with her feet; he was standing in the river-bed and resting his arms on the bridge. "How's tricks? Chris back?"

"No. All is quiet. Come down." He ducked his head and vanished under the bridge. She swung herself down and followed him under the planking. The tunnel in the middle pillar was a grey tube of concrete just tall enough for her to stand up in. Miniature stalactites dripped from the ceiling. Water echoed coolly. Two flat ledges flanked the main water-channel. On one stood the Harp; on the other, Holdfast sprawled. There was a rank smell of mud.

"I got the dust-sheet." She jammed it beside the Harp and sat on it, resting her legs across the channel. "Had to sneak it out. Nosy old pair, me Mum and Dad."

He sat resting his elbows on his knees. "I envy you. Having a home here, I mean. Must be great."

"Envy?" Incredulous. "Good Christ, you don't know what it's like. Hey. You can talk proper."

A smile. "You mean I can talk modern idiom as well as archaic? Naturally. I've wandered out of the Hills enough times to pick *that* up."

"You don't do it round Elathan."

"He doesn't like it."

"He wouldn't. He's not very keen on us, is he? Humans, I mean. Look, can I ask you a personal question?"

"If you like, I don't mind. In fact, I'll ask it for you. You're going to ask me if I'm really elukoi."

"That's right." Holly tried to see if he was annoyed. It didn't seem so. "Are you?"

"Yes and no."

She grinned. "Oh, thanks! No, I mean, you've lived with them, that's obvious. But . . ."

"That's the yes. The no is, I was born human. You know the marsh road? I'm the sole survivor of a pile-up there. Elathan took me into the Hills. I don't remember, I wasn't more than two or three at the time."

"Shit! Oh, 'scuse the language. But I never thought of that."

He shrugged. "That's why I said you're lucky. You can go where you like, do what you like. It's a wide world. But I'm shut in the Hills. I wouldn't have had it any other way; Elathan's been a good father to me. But I want more now."

"Jeez. I'd swop with you any day. Just to get that lot off my back. School an' that. Hey, if you do leave the Hills, never let them get you in a school. If you want to learn there's books, evening classes, day release to college—but not school."

"It's that bad?"

"It's that bad. Look, there's times I lay in bed at night forcing myself to stay awake, so the morning won't come so soon, and I can have just a little longer out of that place. That's how bad it is."

He shifted on the concrete. "I couldn't go now. It would be deserting them. But later—"

"I don't know why you want to leave there. I mean I just *don't*."

"The Hills ... half the things aren't there, are not real. Magic is well enough in its way, but it's all shadow-play and illusion. There's nothing left at the end but dead leaves and dust."

"I don't believe it's really magic."

He glanced up, coming out of the reverie of the Hills. "No, I know you don't."

"Will you leave the Hills?"

"I don't know. There's so much that I don't know. Do you know I can't even read or write English?"

"But—oh. You can in elukoi, I suppose. It couldn't be that different. And you've got time, because you're not planning to go yet ..."

"What?"

"Well, I was thinking. I could teach you. It's only sort of transferring what you know in elukoi into English . . . and I've got books and things." She was waiting for a polite refusal.

"Would you do that?"

"Well, sure. If you want."

"You don't know me."

"I do when you stop playing at being Elathan's messenger boy."

He smiled slowly. "We could arrange time and place—"

"And you could get a job later on—"

Holdfast rolled upright and vanished out of the tunnel. A few seconds later there were footsteps on the bridge and then a heavy scrunch of gravel as Chris jumped down to join them.

"My, aren't we cosy. Shift, you two. Let's get this thing wrapped up before anybody sees it."

Ten minutes saw the Harp wrapped, roped and standing on the path by the bridge. Fletcher squatted by it, adjusting the knots.

"OK," Holly said, out of his hearing, "so we get it up to the road, then what? You don't seriously think they'll let us take it on a bus?"

Chris smiled smugly, infuriating Holly. "Trust me, kid. Chris's got it all arranged. 'S why I was late. What's the time?"

"Twenty to nine. What's arranged?"

"Mmm . . . sunset at half-nine . . . yes. What? Transport's arranged, what else? I got on the phone to Dodo Ogden before I came out. Well, you know her. Buried in a book, but she's always game. Now her brother Ross happens to have a van—is light dawning?"

"Vividly. What did you tell her?"

"I said I had a friend wanted to take his harp up to a renovator in Churchill Road—well, that's the nearest street to Hallows Hill; it only leaves us the marshes."

"Friend?" Fletcher queried.

"You. You're evidence that this is on the level. I told Dodo you lived this end of London Road, and that we'd be outside waiting."

"Oh, Christine!"

Holly laughed. "You're a bloody incredible liar!"

"That's right, and a twenty-four carat genius as well. Now move it."

The van rattled, banged, bumped and jolted its way up to Hallows Hill, and finally pulled up at the junction of Churchill Road and Ashmore Street, on the Surcombe side of the railway bridge.

"Suit?"

"Sure; thanks, Ross. Hate to drag you out, but you know how it is . . ." While Chris leaned on the driver's side of the van and chatted, Holly, Fletcher, and Dodo unloaded the Harp.

"You want any more help?" Dodo pushed her glasses more firmly on her nose. She was a short plump girl some two years younger than Holly, and she wore pink jeans and a white sweat-shirt. Dark blonde hair cut short and scruffy framed a round face. "I'm not doing anything to-night."

Holly prevaricated. "It's only from here to the end of the road. Thanks, but it's not worth your while."

"Aw, OK. You can tell me later what you're really up to."

"Do what?"

"Oh, don't worry, not yet. Finish whatever it is you're doing. But I didn't hoik Ross out of the garage on a Saturday just to listen to one of Chris Ivy's fairy stories."

Holly nodded, noncommital. She thought: Fairy stories! If you only knew.... She remembered that, once out of a book, Dodo was a smart kid.

Chris finished talking, and a chorus of thanks and farewells sent the van on its way.

"Time?" Holly looked down from the bridge to the marshes; a long slope with no cover.

"Coming up for twenty past. We ought to just make it."

They got the Harp over into the field, and then had to rest. Holly stared round in exhaustion. The modern town, busy and dusty, lay on her left; on her right the silence of the marshes and the Downs. In front, the sea took up all the southern horizon, turning sullenly dark under the gliding shadows of clouds. The horizon was sharp indigo, save where the sun dipped low and laid a glittering path across the water. Surf grumbled. The sea was rising.

"It is well that we covered the Harp. Look." Fletcher pointed to gulls wheeling between the sea and the marsh. "They have seen, but may do nothing now."

Holly noted he had reverted to elukoi ways. There was a fierce triumph in him. She and Chris shared it for a moment: the realisation of success.

I never thought we'd do it. Oh, I'd like to see Elathan's face when we turn up with this. Throw us out, would he? We'll show *him*.

In that second she was convinced all would go well; they would deliver up the Harp, Mathurin would play, the Hollow Hills would stand against the sea-people, Eilunieth would recover, the Starlord would come . . .

Holdfast, who had kept close and quiet in the van, loped down into the field and barked.

"Seek out the rest to help me; Greyeyes, if she be there, and Starkweather." He knelt to check the knots as the hound sped away.

"We could get it down there on our own, surely?" Chris was troubled. "Is it OK to let them know?"

"Someone must move the Harp; it may not be a human." He had retreated into an elukoi reserve. "Did you think there would be any but elukoi at the summoning? We are in your debt and I will tell all, but go now. I'll come later and bear news. Go now."

11

Midsummer

"Are you telling us to go *now*? After all we've bloody well done?" Chris was so angry she couldn't say anything else.

Fletcher said quietly, "There's a storm coming up from the sea. Tanaquil Seahawk seeks to know if we are strong enough to send it back. When the Starlord comes, we will be. Watch for a clear sky. I'll come later."

Chris stalked away, her face tight. Holly followed. After a minute she asked, "Where are we going?"

"I don't know. As far from here as I can get. I'm gonna catch the first bloody bus that comes along, and I don't care *where* it's going."

It was a number 447 bus and it took them straight to the Old Town.

"Wonder how long before we know?"

"Shouldn't be long." Holly tilted her head back. The clouds were no longer passing, but massing darkly overhead. The sun still held clear, westering low down on the sea. It was a sultry and uncomfortable evening. "Anyway, what we gonna do?"

"I dunno—what d'you wanna do?"

"Hang around, I guess."

Holly's disappointment had passed. She began to feel almost noble. She thought that not many people would so unselfishly leave the scene of their triumph ... at which point she snorted with laughter, having realised it was a choice between going or being thrown out again. She did not tell Chris what amused her.

"It wasn't his fault, you know."

"Who, Fletcher?" Chris frowned, then conceded, "No, I guess not. He just does what Elathan tells him."

"You reckon?"

"He does. He's got no guts."

"You're only saying that because you're narked."

They paused at the junction of South Street with the seafront. Chains of neon looped from the lamp-posts, pale against the sunset. Out of the mainstream of the crowd, they leaned against the wall by the amusement arcade, listening to the squeals and laughter, the clink of machines and money.

"Think we managed that pretty well, don't you? I ask you, though; harps and magic."

Holly turned from the lights, caught the expression of wry disgust on Chris's face. Her fine fair hair had gone into sweaty tendrils across her damp forehead, and she had undone the top two buttons of her blouse. It was oppressive . . .

"Thought you were the one that didn't believe in magic?"

"I don't. I worked it out in their terms, that's all. I 'spect they went through the caverns so fast they didn't even see the Harp. Or else the morkani have something scientific that no one else has."

"Scientific—" Holly shook her head. You use that word like a talisman. Then she was aware of laughter behind her.

"Ah, look who's here. Aren't they effin' sweet?"

"Bloody hell." Chris groaned under her breath. "That's all I need. Gabriel."

Not only Helen Gabriel, Holly noted, but Diane Cooper

as well, her thin face alive with malicious excitement. She
and Gabriel pushed either side of Holly and Chris, blocking
their way. Gabriel cocked her head sideways; a bullfighter
considering the first thrust—where would it hurt most?

To Holly: "What you down 'ere for? Come to draw more
of your pretty little pictures?"

Cheap bitch. Cheap. Holly noted her tight fashionable
clothes. Like she is. Hell. How do we get out of this?

"There's only two of 'em." Chris—a whisper.

"Let's get lost, we don't want trouble."

"Sugar that. I ain't running."

Gabriel grinned, tried again. "The holly an' the ivy . . .
whatcha doing down this way? You gone on the game,
have you?"

"Why, are we on your beat?" Pleased with her own wit,
Chris added, "There's a funny smell round here, Holly. I
think it's the rats . . ."

The tall girl smiled sickly-sweet, nudged Diane and the
two vanished into the amusement hall. Holly bit her lip.

"Something tells me the rest of her lot's in there—maybe
that biker gang she goes round with. Shall we scat?"

"What the bloody hell for?"

"Look, Chris, you wanna be around to meet Fletch, don't
you?"

" . . . I guess. Hell! Why'd that bitch hafta be here? OK.
Go back and up behind the church; wait on the West Hill."

They retraced their steps up South Street. The Old Town
was growing noisier, raucous music spilling from open
pub doors; holiday voices resounding across the narrow
street. A sudden wind brought Holly the familiar warm smell
of stale beer and cigarette smoke. Above the slate roofs
the storm light grew yellower, and the shadows inched
eastwards.

Just before the church Chris caught Holly's arm, steering her on up the road.

"Don't look back. When I say, we'll scoot round the corner and nip over the churchyard wall. Lay low and they'll lose us."

"Gabriel?" Fear clenching fist-like in her gut, heated with a slow anger.

"Her, Cooper, Cath, couple o' fellas. 'Bout thirty feet behind and coming up fast—OK, go!"

"Christ, that girl, that bloody girl—"

"Go!"

Holly forced herself into a heavy-legged run. Feet clattered behind as they turned up Church Road, and she heard Gabriel's excited shout. Then they were round the corner and briefly out of sight.

Chris vaulted the low stone wall a yard ahead of Holly, turned and pulled her down behind one of the lichenous flat-topped tombs. Holly pressed herself flat in the long grass, shaking with fury. She thought, How dare they? How dare they?

She hardly breathed. In the road she heard a shuffle of feet, then voices.

"The little sods, they've gone." Helen Gabriel.

"Up the passage?" A voice Holly didn't know.

"Ah, leave it. 'S not worth the fuss." Another unknown, male.

"Shaddap, you. OK, check the passage an' the road. They ain't far. Then we'll go—if I say so. God, I hate them. But I can get 'em on Monday. I'll bloody smash 'em."

Departing footsteps. Chris and Holly did not move. Helen spoke.

"Hang about, Di. They're hid up someplace here, I bet."

"Jesus, girl! Drop it, can't you?"

"Sod off. I got an idea."

Holly heard a foot scrape on stone, then the swish of parting grass. Chris's voice was no more than a warm breath by her ear:

"Only two. Get out 'fore the rest come back."

"I'm with you. When?"

"Now!"

Holly sprang up and scrambled over the tomb, Chris beside her. She landed, stumbled, was caught by Diane, pushed past her and then skidded to an agonised halt, with the girl's fist knotted in her hair. She lashed back with her foot, felt a solid contact, and was free.

Shouted obscenities, a scuffle: Chris with Diane.

In front of her now, Helen, half-crouching, arms wide. She hesitated, but fear made her vicious. She slammed a foot at the girl's stomach—Gabriel dodged, took it on the hip—they closed and fell in a tangle.

Got her! Holly knew she was better at wrestling.

A fist drove at her stomach. She blocked it. Gabriel caught both her wrists and bore down. They went flat in the grass, damp earth pressing between Holly's shoulder-blades. Helen's face obscured her vision; cheek, lip, open panting mouth and uneven teeth, no more than inches away. She could only see one eye; thickly mascara'd lashes, a line of pale blue eyeshadow blurred by sweat; the eye itself expressionless because so close.

One foot scraped her shin. She hooked her own legs round Gabriel's; they strained against each other. The girl's head dipped lower. Holly pulled her face away from the frizzy perfumed hair. She could get no purchase.

Helen grunted, unable to free herself. Holly, in a spasm of hate, moved her head an inch and bit down hard on Gabriel's shoulder. The girl winced, swung her head sideways and Holly let go, stunned, seeing the wet imprint of her mouth on the blue cotton.

"You bitch!" She pressed up but still got no leverage. Helen's head dropped out of her line of vision. She felt warm breath on her neck, then the skull grinding her collarbone as Gabriel writhed forward and freed her legs. She felt a knee on her ribs, then it slid to her stomach and drove in hard.

She arched twice, convulsively, like a landed fish and threw the girl bodily off her. Violence drained out of her, leaving only impotent hate.

"I'll *get* you—"

Holly froze, half-sitting, watching the inevitable happen. Gabriel, rolling away, came up hard against the railings of a grave. Pencil-thin railings, but iron; rusted through at the base, and loose.

And the girl came upright with the length of iron in her hand, swinging it round like a stick, in a hard, fast arc. Holly heard the hiss as it cut the air and jerked back as it spanged viciously off a headstone.

A chip of marble grazed her forehead. The blow had left a white scar down the stone itself. Holly, empty-handed, panicked and scrambled up to run. Her heel caught in the knotted grass and she sprawled flat on her back again, knocked breathless, as Helen's arm swung up—

It cut through the air, through the noise of traffic and her own yell; keen and clear and loud. A wild note, it was: a calling and a summons, beating in the air round them. Gabriel let the railing fall and clapped her hands over her ears. Holly caught her breath, had tears in her eyes; she knew beyond all doubt that this was the Harp of Math played by a master, and that nothing called by this could fail to answer.

It ended; the world came slowly back. Holly, seeing

Gabriel's white face, thought, She heard it—but did she hear what we did?

The dark-haired girl lowered her hands, swaying a little, staring blankly past Holly. She licked her lips but did not speak.

Holly was out of the churchyard in a second, feet pounding the road, aware that Chris was beside her. In the High Street she stopped, wrenching air into her lungs, her anger subsiding. Chris stood with her, silently, trying to button her blouse. The top three buttons had been torn off. In the confusion of her pockets Holly found a safety-pin to give her.

She heard a hollow rumble and saw an electric flicker out to sea. As she looked up between the houses she saw a white gull under-skimming the darkness, and all the gaps between the lurid clouds shut up like mouths. The sun was swallowed up as rain began to fall, leopard-spotting the dusty street.

She barely recognised Chris's voice when she said, "It didn't work. The Starlord didn't come."

12

The Sea is Rising

They waited an hour but there was no sign of Fletcher.

Holly rubbed stringy wet hair out of her face, the rain soaking through her thin shirt. The shop doorways and awnings were crowded with scantily-clad tourists. She could see little through the slanting rain and heard only the breath hissing in her throat, and the drains gulping the water down greedily.

When it eased, Chris said, "Let's go home. Nothing's going to happen."

Holly thought she was right. "I wish I could see them. What went wrong? That's what I want to know."

"How do I know? I reckon this Fyraire Starlord of theirs is just another legend that didn't come off. He can't come, or he's dead, or never existed. In which case it's like Elathan says, we've been wasting our time."

"Fyraire . . ."

"What's the matter?"

"Somebody just walked over my grave. God, it's cold."

Chris raised her eyebrows. She thought it a hot and muggy storm. Dismissing it, she said, "Elathan was right—they should've knocked hell out of the sea-people at the first opportunity."

"They'll *have* to now, won't they?"

The rain pelted down in the twilight. A short way away the sea thundered.

"Chris, I'm just gonna go up Tackleway, up the steps, I can see across to the marshes from there."

"What good will that do?"

"None. But I just want to see."

"Well, go up then. I don't care."

Holly climbed the slippery steps. Coming to the top step, the storm hit her full-face, blasting in over the cliffs. It was a sea of gorse and mud there, high enough to catch the last yellow dusk.

What am I doing? I'll go back. Chris was right. She hugged herself, getting wetter. Streaming hair whipped into her eyes. She stepped forward on to Highrock, peering forward to see if she could just glimpse the marsh—

—swayed and slipped and felt rock hit her palms and held it!

She was on one knee, dizzy-headed, with no memory of how she got there. She tried to think.

I was ... everything was different ... sun ... no rain. I saw— no, that's crazy!

It seemed to her as if the rain and the town had been wiped out, and in their place was level ground; a forest of silver birches glittering leafless, red bracken massing over their roots. The sky was not dark but frosty blue, and bright ... For a second she had wanted to run blindly forward into that spring and morning country—and then whatever rift had opened between the worlds closed, and she was wind-beaten and wet and standing on the East Hill. The sea boomed.

She ran pell-mell down the steps away from Highrock, back to the town. Chris glanced up disinterestedly.

"Well?"

"Nothing."

"I thought not. Let's go home."

Holly got off the bus at Birchdale Junction and ran down
Stonegate Street. It was not a late hour to come home; she
didn't anticipate anything more than a scolding for getting
wet.

And who can help being caught in a storm? Especially at
midsummer when you don't expect it. Midsummer—oh,
Jesus, what went wrong?

With her hand on the front gate, she stopped and heard
a groan that was half scream, half shriek, coming from the
field—from the stables. She listened tensely, gripping the
gate, and when it came again, recognised it as a horse. She
ran into the house.

"Oh, you did get caught, didn't you, dear? Couldn't
you find a place to shelter? Come in and take those wet
clothes off."

"OK, Mum. Got this way trying to catch a bus. Hey,
what the hell is that?"

"Next-door said to me it was that white mare foaling. Do
you want a hot drink?"

"Yes please. You mean Strawberry?"

"If that's its name. The vet's van has been down there
for an hour or more now. I hate to hear an animal in pain;
I do wish he'd do something for it . . ."

As her mother vanished into the kitchen, the scream came
again. Holly pulled off shirt and shoes and jeans and began to
scrub herself dry with a towel.

"Good Lord, girl, what happened to you? You look like
a drowned rat."

"Hi, Dad; I got caught in the rain down the Old Town.
See that lightning?"

"Don't catch cold. Go up and put a dressing-gown on."

"OK, OK: don't fuss."

The sound of the mare's torment did not fade until midnight was past. Warm in bed, with the rain clawing the windows, Holly lay down and cried herself to sleep.

She heard the rain stop around six and then drifted through troubled dreams in the darkness, and overslept. It was close on ten before she woke again.

The grey slate roofs gleamed silver, the trees sparkled, and coils of mist drifted over the pond in the park. Holly dragged herself out of bed and pulled the window open, hearing church bells. The plants in the garden were flattened; the horse's field a ploughed morass. She saw two men come out of the stables and plod across to a van parked in the drive, and heard their voices clearly:

"She'll be fine now. I can't answer for the foal. I'll drop by again later."

"I don't understand it. It looks as if—"

The van's engine coughed noisily. Holly put her head in her hands, hating the morning. That Strawberry should have trouble now seemed only natural. There isn't much lately that hasn't gone wrong, she thought.

Chris was at church, she knew, so she went alone to the ruins of Orionë. The rocks were damp and ominous; more of the bank had come down with the storm. No Fletcher. Not even Holdfast.

She thought, He's somewhere. He said he'd let me know what happened, and he wouldn't let me down. I can't go to the Hills . . .

She caught one of the infrequent Sunday buses down to the Old Town, but the boy was not at Highrock, as she'd half-hoped he would be. She wandered down the deserted streets, listening to the muffled singing coming from the churches. The morning was clear. She thought, If the sea-people are controlling the weather they're not very good at it. Or have they made their point, and are they saving all their strength for midwinter?

She walked back along the promenade towards the town centre. Thinking hard and not looking where she was going, she apologised automatically when she bumped into someone coming from the opposite direction.

"Christ! What you doin' down here?"

It was Helen Gabriel alone, without her gang.

"Where's Ivy, then?"

"Search me." Holly was not intimidated. She barely remembered how the other girl had tried to hurt her.

"That, last night. What was it?"

A civil question? Holly wondered. The hell. She's curious. "You mean in the churchyard? What did it sound like to you?"

"Like . . . I dunno what like. Nothing clear. Too bright." She shook her head impatiently; the moment of understanding passed. "Look, one of you poxy little cows knows what it was, and you're bloody well gonna tell me!"

"Keep off me, Gabriel." Holly walked away, felt a hand slam into her shoulder and staggered, thinking, Just let her try! I'll beat shit out of her.

"Don' you play tough with me, girl."

"Stay off me," she snapped back, then: "because you don't know what'll happen if you don't . . ."

At any other time Helen would have laughed scornfully, and hit her. Now she stared at Holly for a long minute, then pushed past and walked away, not looking back.

Holly went home.

She didn't see Fletcher the next day, or the day after that;

and then it lengthened into weeks. With the end of the summer term and the prospect of two weeks camping in Cornwall, Holly put the Hills to the back of her mind. When she came back from Cornwall and met up with Chris, there was the park, the cinema, the beach; tennis, swimming, and the pure joy of being off school and doing nothing at all. A whole month.

August drew to a close in the hottest summer that century. Since they were due back at school on the next Tuesday, Holly and Chris came down to the beach on the Saturday for one last long afternoon.

Chris picked her way round trippers, towels, deck chairs, and transistor radios to settle down in the shelter of a stone breakwater. Holly, barefoot, winced over the pebbles.

Voices and music jarred in the sweltering heat. Acres of blue sky burned above. The promenade was packed with people. All wore shirtsleeves, or light summer dresses, or swimming costumes. They covered the beach like ants. The hotels and boarding-houses along the seafront wavered in the heat-haze. Ice-cream sellers sold out.

Holly paused, removing her jeans. A worn red swimming costume showed underneath. She said, "Are we safe near the sea?"

"You what?" Chris was nonplussed for a minute, then, "Not that again. Look, we're out of it. We'd've heard if it was otherwise, in two an' a half months."

"Yes, but I just thought—"

"You worry too much. If you wanna worry about anything, try Gabriel. You reckon she's gonna be all sweetness and light after last term?"

"Do I, hell!"

"Well, then. Come *on*."

Holly made sure she could keep an eye on her clothes,

then ran down over the pebbles to the hard-packed sand, where fan-like ripples inched up the beach.

Holly waded out, ankle, knee, thigh-deep; cold as charity; then struck out and let the sea hold her, rolling with the waves. The chill wore off as she swam out, floated, and let the translucent water thrust her shorewards. She drifted, feet just touching the sandy bottom. Chalkspit had vanished in haze; it was as if the world ended at Gallows Hill . . .

At last she waded ashore, stomach queasy with swallowing salt water. Out of the sea her limbs were stone-heavy. She sat on the towel and let the heat ease her and dry her stinging eyes. She fell into a half-trance.

Shouting roused her. She blinked stupidly, not realising what she was seeing, and then it came into focus. Chris, out of her depth, clinging to the slippery stone groin and screaming. Then losing hold and going under so smoothly it was a second before Holly jumped up and ran down the beach.

She stopped. Stared helplessly at the shining and empty sea. No telling where . . .

Bare feet slapped the stone behind her. A boy, running down the breakwater, sure-footed where the waves beat across it. She knew it was Fletcher. He knelt astride the stone where Chris had vanished, and reached down. He was shouting, but not in English, and not at Holly. She waded out to try and help.

"Get back!"

"What?"

"Get back, quick. I've got her." He waved her back with one hand, the other shoulder-deep in the sea.

Holly splashed ashore. In all that crowd she saw no one taking any notice of them. They think we're mucking about. Good God, no wonder people drown.

Chris stumbled up the shingle, supported by Fletcher. Holly caught her as she staggered, and sat her down on the towel. The girl was a sick white, gold hair sleaked dark, water pearling her face and body. She was staring vacantly at the sea and shaking.

Fletcher squatted down. "You have a drink for her?"

"What? Yeah, somewhere. We had a flask of coffee." She let Chris have a cup, and the girl drank it down scalding hot. "What happened? There ain't no rocks. Was it cramp? I never seen anything like that—"

Chris pulled the towel up round her shoulders. She focused on Holly and Fletcher, and tried to smile.

"Never learn, do you?" The boy sat back on his heels. Holly saw he was in jeans and T-shirt, his hair longer, his skin dark. Although he still had a slight accent, his phrasing was entirely human.

Chris pushed the wet hair out of her eyes, and was herself again. "God, that was bad. You won't believe what I saw—"

"I might," Fletcher invited.

"Well. I was just mucking around, floating. Somebody grabs my ankle and pulls me down—I think it's some yob, so I kick out, but he don't let go. So I go under, swallow some water, get scared. Thought I could hold on the breakwater. He pulls me down. Then I see him."

"Underwater?" Holly interrupted.

"I could see enough. He was breathing. Under water. And the way he looked; My God, vicious. I couldn't swear to it—but I think his fingers were webbed."

I know how Chris loves to exaggerate . . . but no, she was really scared. Holly asked, "Sea-people?"

Fletcher pointed upwards at the white blizzard of wings, and they listened to the harsh crying. "They finally found you. And Tarac's people don't dare come this close to the sea."

"Lucky you were around."

"I've been watching you since midsummer."

"Watching—?"

He said, "I suggest you get off the beach. I told the seaborn to leave you be, or I'd set the hounds on him. If we wait too long he'll find out I was lying. All right?"

"All right." As they prepared to go, Holly asked, "Where's Holdfast, then?"

"In the Hills."

"He didn't come with you?"

He was facing the sea, so she couldn't see his face when he said, "I haven't been in the Hills since midsummer."

13

Autumn

Ten minutes later the three of them were leaning on the rail at the bus-stop waiting for a bus to Birchdale Junction. Away from the open sea, the buildings shut in the heat. The town was furnace-hot, smelling of dust and petrol and sweat.

"So what happened midsummer?" Holly persisted.

"Nothing," Fletcher said. "Do you think, if anything had happened, the morkani would dare come that close to the shore?"

"What went wrong?"

He sighed. "I don't know. Starkweather and I brought the Harp to Mathurin, and him white with relief, but he played. And there was Elathan, Oberon, the House of Raven ... and he hit the note, I swear it; the note that breaks the walls between the worlds—"

"We heard it," Chris told him.

"So you know what it was like. I think we broke through for a second—I saw another place. Trees and bracken."

Holly looked up quickly. "*I* saw that."

"Yes. Yes, there might be a few humans who could. But it does not matter, the Starlord did not hear. That's all. There's nothing else."

"Yeah, but ..." Holly paused, studying him, thinking, He's different, how? He doesn't look younger than me, not now. "You said you weren't in the Hills?"

He was sullen. "All I asked Elathan to do was trust me. We know one of the elukoi is traitor—I didn't want them to know how we got the Harp. So I didn't tell. He said if I felt that way I need not come back to the Hills. I said—" he stopped on an intake of breath, shaking his head at the memory "—I said a lot. And walked out."

Jesus! Holly was swamped with envy. If only we could all do that—!

"Both of you; one more thing. Ignore any contact from the Hills. It would be a morkani trick—or if not, they'd want to find me. And I'm not interested."

Chris was on a different track. "You got nowhere to stay, then?"

"I've been sleeping in those caves up the East Hill."

"They stink." Chris added, "And what about winter? If you're staying permanent, you'll want a job, too."

"I've met some people who might help me."

Holly put in, "Yes, but you need a place to stay in the meantime. Listen, Chris, you know the horse's field; there's two stables and a shed. I dunno what it's like now, but last year the man had it done up as accommodation, so he could come down and spend the night if one of the horses was sick. There's water and electric. The old man that owns it, he's crackers, got pots of money. Now suppose—"

"I'm ahead of you. But what about when they come to look at the horses?"

"That's just it, that's what put the idea into my head. There was only Strawberry and her foal there, and they've moved them over to the Hollington stables, and shut these up for the winter. So it's free till spring, March at least. What d'you think, Fletch?"

"Oh, you are going to ask me? I did wonder. Yes, I

don't see why not. As for a job—" a questioning glance at Holly.

"We'll work something out." She would have him close at hand, she realised, and be able to tell him what he needed to get on.

"Hey-up, here's the bus." Chris tucked her towel under her arm and felt in her pockets. "Who's got bus fare?"

They drifted apart around six, Fletcher having seen the shed and agreed that it was habitable. Holly expected to find her parents home, as they had decided to skip the visit to Combe Marish.

She thought, Maybe we can have a proper Saturday evening. We haven't since that old goat got ill. He won't get better and he won't die—what can you do?

Shutting the front door behind her, she knew at once that something was wrong. For a wild moment she thought the attack on Chris had been a diversion, while something reached out to this house from the sea . . .

A door banged. Her mother came downstairs, the familiar harassed expression on her face. Seeing Holly, she stopped.

"What's up? Where's Dad?"

"He's on his way over to Combe Marish, dear."

But Holly already knew, and thought she must have known since she came in. "Grandad's dead, then?"

"Your father had a call from Elizabeth. He went into hospital again on the Wednesday and died last night. Daddy's gone over to be with Elizabeth." She drew a deep breath, let it out slowly, and walked down the rest of the stairs. "Well, we expected it sooner or later."

Yeah, but this is sooner. Holly's skin had gone clammy-cold and she felt violently sick.

The funeral took place the following Monday.

The cold and sickness in her increased all through that Monday morning, though the temperature was in the eighties. She was silent during the short drive to Combe Marish, and it took an effort to follow her parents into the house.

"At three." Her father's voice. "Cremation."

Holly stared out of the window, yearning for the sunlight, praying for the end of the day. Her thoughts were chaotic. I'm so scared, so afraid. I never thought it was going to happen ... I never meant what I said. If he could die, anybody could. Never believed that. Anybody. Liz, Dad, Mum—even them, Even me. Oh God, even me ...

Two long black cars came, one with flowers and the pale wood coffin, one for the family. Holly banged her head getting into the car, flushed with embarrassment, held back an obscenity. At other times there would have been a laugh to take the sting out of it, but now—father, mother, aunt; all locked in the same silence.

The coffin's so small, I didn't think it'd be like that ... She pulled her thoughts away from it. This car smells of leather. It's so hot. Can't we have a window open ... suppose not. We're going fast. I always thought these things were slow. Maybe it's a long way. Let me out of here!

Cold and sweating again, she dragged her mind away from panic. Her father sat beside her with bowed head. She thought: Never crossed my mind—he was his father. How would I feel if Dad—no! Hell. He must feel terrible.

On impulse she put her hand over his and squeezed it. He lifted his head and smiled briefly. She smiled back, then leaned against the black upholstery, partially reassured.

The Sussex countryside glided past, parched with the long heat. Most of the way ran through narrow high-hedged country lanes, where yellow leaves foreshadowed autumn.

At last the cars slowed and turned and glided smoothly up the drive to the crematorium.

"You go in with Elizabeth, dear."

"What?" Hearing her mother's whispered instruction, Holly nearly backed out completely. "Hey, no, not me—"

"Go on! I'm not telling you twice!"

Holly went.

There was a building which she supposed must be a chapel, though the inside was very modern. A dark-suited man played an organ quietly.

How many times does he do *that* in a day? She wondered. It's just a job to them, I suppose. What a way to make a living.

A young clergyman officiated. Holly fumbled her way into the pews by Elizabeth and watched him while the others settled. Brown eyes, brown hair, not bad-looking, too old . . . She watched the light slant down through high windows. . . . I suppose that thing over there is a bier . . .

The coffin stood on a raised platform to their left, between pews and altar. Holly looked once, then avoided it.

The words of the service went over her head, she paid no attention. It was difficult enough to watch out of the corner of her eye and see what her parents did; to kneel when they did, stand and sit when they did, and—final embarrassment —join her feeble voice with theirs when they sang one verse of a hymn. The coffin glided out of sight behind a curtain, to accompanying chords from the organ.

Let me out! She had shut herself off from everything with that thought, repeating it over and over inside her head to drown out all other thoughts. Now it was over. She stood a little distant from the group while the clergyman talked with her aunt and her parents. She saw Elizabeth had been crying, was red-eyed and white-faced. There was a quick discussion about whether the flowers should go to the local hospital or not ...

Out in the open air at last, Holly stretched and flung back her head and let all the tension drop away from her. The sun slanted gold in her face. The last trees of summer glowed green against the hot pale blue sky; a breeze shook the trees and brushed her face; she heard distant cars and the quarrelling of sparrows. Beyond the trees the country unrolled patchwork to the horizon; dark hedges, clustered villages, needle-spires; and the great fields of corn, golden, ash-white, pale as snow. Smoke rose from other fields; stubble being burnt off, and the acrid biscuity smell came to her clearly. The world was brilliant as crystal and running over with light.

Suddenly her throat was tight, she must open her mouth to breathe; tears were stinging in her eyes as she stood struck through by summer, and all the coldness fell from her.

What a day! It sang in her head, still with her face to the wind and the light; seeing and feeling and touching and smelling the world. It was pure joy to stand four-square on the earth in a young and healthy body. She wanted to run and run forever, leap high and come down wild and yelling—

Her mother's touch recalled her and she stooped to enter the car again. The others followed, less silent, more relaxed. It's over, the worst is over ... they talked quietly and without tension.

For the first time Holly's thoughts went to her grandfather as a person, not a sick object or a horror in a pine box. She thought, I didn't like him when he was alive and I won't say I do now he's dead, but Lord! am I sorry for him. All this, all the world—I can see it, he can't, and never will again. He's dead, that's that. But me ... as long as you're alive and healthy, as long as it can be like this—what else matters? What else could?

Holly and Chris met in the playground, in the crowd surrounding the blackboard with the new form-lists on it.

"We still together?"

Chris elbowed her way to the front. "Anderson, H; Ivy, C; ye gods above—"

"Gabriel, H?"

"You said it, kid. Most of her lot, too—they don't seem to have switched many people this time. And we're in Hut Five—"

"Not the Huts again!" In winter the five prefab classrooms were draughty, cold and cramped.

"—with guess who, your friend and mine, Taf Jones the historical hysterical Welshman."

Holly shrugged. "Taf's OK. I might stand a chance of passing history if we've got him for form-master."

"Only if the O-level's on Owen Glendower!"

"Let's shift up and grab desks before the rabble get in there."

They extricated themselves from the crowd and ran up to the Huts. Holly banged her satchel down on the back row corner desk, sat down and put her feet up. She hated the first day of term. Chris put her case on the next desk and leaned on top of it.

"Wanna talk to you."

"Go ahead, I'm all ears—no funny comments required."

Chris ignored the attempted humour. "You free tonight?"

"Sure, sure. Where're we going?"

"Brancaer."

Holly stared blankly for a second, then sighed. "Forget it."

"Forget it, hell! Because of what that boy says? I've been thinking—"

"Don't. You'll strain something."

"Never mind all that. There's too many things we don't know about. . . . We're not safe. Last Saturday proved that."

"Don't be dramatic."

"Dammit all to hell, somebody tried to *kill* me—now don't you make faces at me, Holly Anderson, you know damn well that what I say is true!"

"So there's a very simple answer. Leave it alone."

"Think we can? Come midwinter there's going to be trouble with a capital T. Think it'll only be the Hills? Think the sea-people won't remember us?"

"Well. . . ." I don't want to get involved again, but . . . "Say what you like, Fletcher had good reasons for warning us off."

"Just because him and Elathan have split up. I want to know what the Hills are going to do now."

You're scared. Me too. Holly knew better than to argue directly. "What say we go round to Fletch's after school and see what he says?"

"And if he don't come up with something, we go see Elathan."

"Let's hear the boy first."

The day wore on. Above the town birds flew singly or in flocks, patrolling or watching. Gulls were thick along the shoreline. Sparrows and thrushes perched on roofs in company with Tarac and others of her people.

On the ground was little activity. A cat dozed in the sun by Chris's house, another by Holly's; a third prowled about the school. They also were backed up—one by a dirty mongrel with red ears, whose pups were also waiting about the town.

Stalemate. Let one gull stray too far inland and it was mobbed by carrion crows. Let one hound come too close to the beach and it must run with a dozen razor-beaked gulls to speed it on its way.

Holly and Chris and the rest of the human population of the south coast remained serenely unaware that a war was going on. Only the elukoi and morkani knew and marked each loss.

"Now?"

"OK."

The two girls went over the hedge into the horse's field without being seen. It was shortly after half-past seven, the sun setting slowly. As far as their parents were concerned they were at the Youth Club.

"Meaning we have till at least half-ten," Chris had said, "since they don't chuck out till ten. If we're going to the Hills we need that much time."

"Yeah. *If.*"

Now they went up the margins of the field towards the stables, and the low building that Fletcher was converting for his own use. There were no sounds; the sky was clear of all birds.

"He'll be in, won't he?"

Chris nodded. "Still doing it up."

"Then why's it so quiet—Jesus!"

They stopped simultaneously in front of the shed. Chris stared, bewildered. "What—a—mess!"

"What hit it, a bomb? Fletch! Hey, Fletcher, you there?" Holly peered forward. The double door had been smashed off its hinges and lay discarded in the mud. The garage-sized interior had contained a workbench and a camp-bed; they lay shattered under the broken window. There was no sign of the boy.

"You reckon someone did the place over while he was out?"

"No chance, kid. He had no reason to go out, he was too busy. 'Sides, looks like a fight to me."

Holly picked her way in, carefully avoiding the splintered glass. "If he was here, where is he now? Jesus, what a stink!"

"Hmm, see what you mean: like rotting seaweed. Hey-up."

"What?"

She pointed. A triangular piece of denim was hanging from a nail in the door-frame. "He was here, OK."

They looked at each other, then back at the shambles.

"Chris, d'you think . . .?"

"I don't know. But, Christ, I'm afraid so."

"Same ones as got you."

"The ones out of the sea. Don't ask me how, but that's it. As for why nobody noticed, well, nobody noticed Orionë either. That settles it. We go to the Hills. Now."

He needs help, there isn't anyplace else he'll get it. Holly nodded reluctantly. "The cops—"

"Would lock *us* up as loonies. Now let's move it, before somebody happens along and catches us here."

"Right!"

Holly was so engrossed in thinking what she would say to Elathan that the journey to the Hills passed in a dream. The marshes exuding white mist, bone-chillingly cold; the scarlet and sulphur clouds hiding the sun; the raven-guard that met them, and Silver guiding them over the mud: she barely noticed it. If the morkani *had* got Fletcher . . .

There's nothing we can do, she thought miserably.

Once in Brancaer, the elukoi girl led them through dim grassy ways to Elathan's tower. Up the outer flight of steps —she rapped lightly on the window as she passed it; then stood aside to let them pass through the door first.

Holly, turning her head to look at the yellow candle-lit

windows of Brancaer, cannoned into Chris who'd stopped dead.

"What the—?" She saw past Chris into the room. There were two people sitting by the fire. One was Elathan, his face unreadable. The other; bruised, sulky and subdued—

"Fletcher?"

14

The Hills in Darkness

Holly realised it at once: there had been no attack by the sea-people. But Fletcher was obviously not in the Hills by his own choice.

That only leaves one person, Holly thought, and that's Elathan. Suppose he's going to keep us here? Suppose he's decided he doesn't want anybody knowing about the Hills —ever?

She distrusted the darkness outside the tower window; the candle shadows in the room; the inhuman man and his changeling son. A cold wind lifted the hair on her neck. The Hills had been frightening enough when she'd thought the elukoi were friendly . . .

"I am sorry to bring you here by a trick, but needs must; and there was no other way. Holly, Christine; will you hear me?"

Chris was leaning up against the window-frame, elaborately unconcerned. "So talk," she said.

Elathan stood and began pacing restlessly. "Midwinter comes on us apace. We must fight or go down to the morkani. One great advantage we have—iron. We may forge, work metal; while the sea-folk make do with flint. We overmatch them there."

He paused, then said, "Magic will turn the battle. I will not be falsely modest, I am Master Sorcerer; but I am one alone. The last master of the fifty-seven branches of magic in the Hollow Hills. The morkani have three masters that I know of: Fiorin, Dalziel, and Tanaquil Seahawk, the Hand of Domnu. It may be there are more. Albeit solely those three, matters will not go well with us."

"That's tough," Chris said, as he seemed to want a response. "All the same, what's it got to do with us?"

He faced them.

"You are human: destroy magic wherever you be. So: be with us at midwinter! Then there is *no* magic; neither Hills nor Sea; and so we may meet sword to sword and prove who is the better. What say you?"

Fletcher interrupted before they could speak. "It is not your quarrel. Also, it is not necessary. The Harper speaks against it. The Lady Eilunieth will turn no hand to war. Let the Seahawk's people lay seige to the Hills, and starve at our gate."

"We have not the power to keep that gate against them." Elathan dismissed it. "Now: Christine?"

"I'm thinking—I can't tell you straight off. Us? Are we the last chance?"

"Yes."

She shrugged. "I guess that's us in, then. OK, Holly?"

"No."

"You what?"

It took a moment for it to sink in, she was so used to Holly following her lead.

"No it isn't OK. I'm having nothing to do with this at all. Not because I'm afraid—I am, but that's not why."

Holly, seeing Chris's face, thought, I'm letting her down badly, we always do things together; and I don't even know if I can explain.

She said to Elathan, "You talk about fighting as if it didn't matter, as if it was just fist-fights like me and her get into at school. It *isn't*. People are going to get killed—you know, dead, forever. And maybe it wasn't their idea to get mixed up in it in the first place. Go someplace else, start again. Nothing's worth *dying* for. I've seen it—I know."

Chris grabbed her arm, spiteful, hurting. "Listen, you idiot, we've got to do this to make up—"

"I'm not going to!" She saw Elathan was not very concerned. So. One of us is enough.

"I will have Hawkhunter take you from the Hills, and you wait."

Fletcher pushed his chair back and stood up. "I'll take her myself."

"You will not leave."

The boy shepherded her towards the door, talking all the way. "I agree with Holly—there has to be another way out. Until you find it, I'm going back where I belong."

Elathan swallowed, forcing back anger. "You are my son but you be young as yet. I know the best for you; in time you'll see it also."

"You *used* me—I said at midsummer I'd have nothing to do with this, and I say so now. I know my own mind."

"Son—"

"I'm not your son!"

In the silence Holly heard the branches rasping together outside the window. Nothing else. He's done what I do, she thought, said too much, said what he really means.

"I have brought you up and been as a father to you and this is what you say to me?"

Fletcher hustled her outside and down the stairs. It was raw cold. Dark buildings were fringed with stars, trees loomed. All the constellations were askew.

Holly realised she had lost Brancaer. But Fletcher . . . she thought; and heard in her mind Elathan's final words, half-obliterated by the slamming door "... The Hills' blessing on you, boy."

"Hey—where're you going?"

"Shortest way." Fletcher led her away from the gate, while her head cleared from the dizziness of passing through it, and on over the cold white marsh. She dared not lift her eyes from the treacherous ground. When they reached dry land it proved to be the little-used coast road between Surcombe and Combe Marish.

She thought, That's a better way out of—and into—the Hills, wonder why we didn't use it before. Oh ...

The road lay between two sparsely-hedged banks. Over the farthest she saw the grass give way to shingle, and beyond that a black glimmer of sea. The moon had risen three-quarters full; its light made a greenish patch on the waters. Sea and horizon and sky were one blackness, the world seemed smaller than in the light of day.

"We got nothing to worry about; if we're nothing to do with the elukoi then the same goes for the morkani—so there's nothing to prevent us taking the short way home."

Holly nodded uncertainly. "Yeah. It's only half-nine. We might get a bus if we're lucky. Let's walk and see if we can find a bus-stop."

"Good idea."

They set off towards the town. Two cars went past, leaving a vacuum of silence that the sea filled. Holly wasn't quite sure where they were on the marsh road so she didn't know how far it was to the next bus-stop. Hallows Hill and the slopes beyond it jutted into the night like the backs of fabulous begemmed beasts. A line of fire was reflected in the sea—the neon glare of the pier.

A touch on her shoulder. She saw Fletcher gesture silence, then stop. Listening brought her nothing but sea-sounds and rustles in the hedges.

"What—?"

"Something—or somebody. I can smell sorcery. Surely Elathan wouldn't put a sending on us, not with you here . . ."

The sea-swept marsh was lonely, the road forsaken, and the town lights a million miles away. Holly shivered. A voice spoke out of the darkness ahead, and with fear she realised that it was speaking in the liquid tongue of the elukoi, but it was not a voice she knew.

Fletcher peered into the darkness. He could see only a vague silhouette of something on the bank, something man-like.

"Where are your hounds now, wizard's boy, to set on the people of the sea?"

His first thought was a regret that he no longer had his bow, his second was amazement that the sea-people should be so strong in magic as to come out of the water already.

"Who are you?"

"Fiorin of the House of the Hawk."

"What d'you want?" One of the masters of sorcery, Fletcher thought. Is he armed? How long can he stay out of the water?

"Not so hasty. I had not thought to meet with you here, though I hoped greatly. You can be of use to me, wizard's boy."

"I'm no wizard's brat, or anything to do with the Hills! Leave us be, Master Fiorin. We're human, and we don't mix in your business. There's nothing we could do for you."

He was conscious of the girl beside him shaking his arm.

"Who is it? What does he want?"

He realised Holly would not have understood a word of

their conversation. He tried to make his voice reassuring. "It's one of the morkani. Just stay still for the moment, I'll handle it."

The cold voice spoke again. "Who is that with you, boy? It looks human."

"Nothing to do with you," the boy snapped. "Say what you came to say and let us go on."

"I am not stopping you. So you have left the Hills, and a human is with you—one of the ones I have been watching, if I do not mistake her. Where is the other?"

"No business of yours."

"I think she went into the Hills. I do not know why, I admit. Is your Elathan enlisting human aid against us? No. He knows well enough what happens to mortals in that kind of war. Boy, you do not go from here until you tell me why the elukoi have taken up with humans."

"Run for it," Fletcher said in English, then charged forward. His shoulder hit stone-cold skin; there was a crash. The road fled under their feet. There were syllables shouted into the wind behind them, but they had no effect. When they could run no further they stopped, looking back nervously.

No one followed them.

Fletcher chuckled quietly. "There's one trouble with magic, Holly-girl. You get to depend on it. You forget there are other ways of doing things. If he'd had a blade it might've been very nasty. He wasn't expecting us. He thought magic would be enough. It would've been if you hadn't been there."

"Who was he—*what* was he?"

"Fiorin of the morkani. One of the masters of sorcery. We're gonna be all right. We don't need the elukoi. You'll see."

"Tell me what he was saying." She shivered. "I'm glad I couldn't see him too clearly."

"I'm glad he didn't bring anyone else with him—and that gulls don't see too well in the dark."

Holly was just getting into bed when the phone rang. When her mother called her she grabbed her dressing-gown and clattered downstairs. She wanted it to be Chris; most of all she wanted it to be Chris saying she'd changed her mind.

"Hello?"

"You bloody idiot, what d'you think you were doing tonight?"

"Look, Chris, I *told* you at the time why I'm not going to—"

"I'm not talking about that! You and that stupid boy—are you trying to get all of us killed? Of all the damn stupid—"

"Chris! Slow down. What are you so mad about?"

There was a hissing sigh from the other end of the line.

"You went on the sea road and got mixed up with one of the morkani."

"Yeah. Hey, that was good! I bet he's still wondering why me and Fletch ain't frazzled. Who told you? Tarac, I suppose. Chris, it was the one that tried to get you, the one we met, Fiorin—Fletcher told me that he recognised him—"

"Holly!"

"What?"

"He *won't* still be wondering. That's the point. An idiot could work it out now, knowing what he knows. The morkani wanted to know why there were humans in the Hills, didn't they? Now they've found out we're immune to this so-called magic. You've cocked it up good an' proper this time. Come midwinter they'll be ready and waiting, and they'll know just who to go for first—me!"

15

Home Visit

Half-term passed in a late October of frost, mists and thick drifts of brown leaves. Chris was remote and secretive; she and Holly had no contact outside the lessons they attended together. It bothered Holly, keeping the elukoi constantly in her mind. It was no use talking to Fletcher—he refused to discuss it at all. It was as if he were determined not only to be human, but never to have been anything else.

Holly took up with Dodo Ogden. The bookish girl was amiable; willing to discuss anything from atomic power to Davy Starren, criticise the older girl's style of football, and chatter of her own interest in the horses her father shod. However, being two years younger than Holly, she was not on hand in class to help when Helen Gabriel caused trouble. Gabriel had got over her fright, Holly discovered; if anything she was more vicious.

The evenings darkened and the days grew dim. It sleeted at the end of November. Holly, sitting on the school radiators, cursed Hut Five blasphemously and at length. In the first week of December she came down with such a cold that, when she heard the doctor prescribe a fortnight at home, she was too miserable even to enjoy the absence from school.

She was alone in the house. The cold had dwindled to a sniffle, and she had decided to go back to school the next day.

It was the last day of term then, and she had no intention of missing the class parties or the Christmas play.

The afternoon was dark, though it was only two o'clock. Thick yellow clouds threatened snow, but there was a keen east wind that would keep it from falling yet. Holly turned from the cold glass and its view of wet dark earth and trees; all in twilight.

In front of the fire was a pile of Christmas decorations. She had strung crepe ribbons and holly round the walls, and made a start on the tree; now she wondered whether it was worth starting paper-chains. She pulled her dressing-gown more tightly over her pyjamas. It was a luxury not to dress . . .

A knock at the front door.

She was half inclined to ignore it; the cold had left her apathetic. Whoever it was would go away eventually . . .

Again; this time louder.

Oh hell. She yawned wearily, and wandered out into the hall. The lino was cold; she hoped she wouldn't be kept standing a long time. She opened the door a few inches on the guard-chain.

It was the clothes she recognised; dark coat and dark hat with the brim pulled low—for a second she thought Elathan! and almost slammed the door.

Then he faced her, tipped the hat back, and smiled.

"Mathurin?" She pushed the door to and slipped the chain, then opened it fully. "Come on in. What's happened?"

"Nothing bad. Just harper's curiosity." He went into the sitting-room, slung his hat on the table, and stretched out leisurely in the chair. Holly cleared a pile of tinsel out of the way and sat beside him.

"What're you curious about, then?"

"How you fare, you and the boy. Is there trouble?"

"No ... we wondered why not. I mean, the sea-people know what you and Chris plan to do. I wonder they're not after her; and us too."

He sat back, shadow sliding across the narrow planes of his face. Beast-eared, red-haired, golden-eyed ... he was more wild and real than she remembered. And here he was in her own house.

"They have tried. But then, magic fails them there. And we be strong enough to beat their creatures off. Themselves, they cannot come ashore for more than moments yet; though that may change soon."

"Why bother defending me and Fletch?"

"You did not ask to be concerned in this. It was chance we found him. Chance it was that put you near the Hawk-coin. Truly, it's no concern of yours."

"No ..." Holly was unsure. "You said the sea-people may change?"

A grave golden stare. "Three days from now, it is mid-winter. Had you forgot?"

"I'd tried." She got up, nervous, changing the subject. "Would you like a cup of coffee?"

"What's coffee?"

I still keep forgetting. After all this time, I keep expecting them to be like us ... "It's a drink made out of roast beans. You might like it. I'll put the kettle on."

He followed her out to the kitchen, looking up the stairs as he went. It was obvious that 17 Stonegate Street was as strange to him as Brancaer had been to her.

"If the sea-people win, what then?" Automatically her hands dealt with the percolator while her thoughts were elsewhere.

"I know not. An they take the Hills, it may be they'll settle content—it may be not. I'd warn the boy to move away. An you've a place in another town, I'd go there." He shrugged. "And they may lose."

"I should let that coffee get cooler before you try it." She thought, Is he trying to persuade me—us—to go back? If so—nothing doing.

They returned to the fire.

"How's the boy doing?"

"OK. He's got a job in the same garage as Ross Ogden —that's the brother of a friend of mine. Don't know how he swung that one; but he can sure look after himself."

"And still lives in that hut?"

"For the moment. He's reckoning to look for a flat in the New Year. I wish I'd got the independence he has."

"Has he?"

"Yes." Holly was determined. "He doesn't owe the Hills anything."

"You and he have still the same opinion, there's no chance you'll return to us?"

"Not a snowflake's chance in hell—is that what you came for?"

"Partly." He sipped the coffee and made a face. After a second's consideration he downed the rest of it and smiled. "Got any more of that?"

"Sure. Hang about." There was still boiling water in the kettle. She thought, Suppose they lose because of me? Oh but I couldn't make that much difference, not one person. And they've got Chris. And they don't *have* to fight . . .

Back by the fire again, with winter darkening around them: "Does Chris go to the Hills often?"

She saw he looked concerned.

"Do you not know?"

"I know she goes there. But she don't talk about it."

"I see. Yes. She comes often."

Her coffee was stone cold. "Is she going to be enough?"

"If that were known for certain, all would be happier. No, that is a lie—for myself. I would she were of your mind. If that were so, and midwinter surely lost, then mayhap Elathan would be less willing to begin a slaughter. But he holds the honour of the Hills to be one with his own honour."

Holly grunted, and shook her head. "I don't know."

"Nor I."

She had questions, most of them irrelevant, but she felt this might be her last contact with the elukoi.

"That Hawk-coin . . . it's just the pattern that bothered me. I've been thinking, and it was a bit different from the others round the well." Seeing his puzzlement, she stood up. "I made a sketch of it; I'll show you."

He studied it for some minutes in silence. She fidgeted.

"It wouldn't make any difference now, I suppose? Did we ought to tell Elathan?"

Mathurin leaned back. "That is no coin of the Well."

"No—well, what *is* it?"

"I have seen few of these, but they are the Great Seals, the sigils of each House of Faerie. This, from the form, was a sigil of the House of the Hawk; see, here is Tanaquil . . ." his claw-nailed finger tapped the paper.

"But if it didn't come from the Well?"

"Then from where?" He frowned. "The morkani do not come on land; besides, this was afore midsummer. Therefore it was given to an elukoi—that elukoi who is traitor to us all. And if it were lost . . ."

"It'd be a dead give-away," Holly concluded. "So I guess this person wanted to cover it up. And they put the blame on a Well-coin, so that no one would connect it with the morkani. Is that right?"

"It may be."

"But what would he or she be doing in the Old Town?"

Mathurin picked up the drawing again, studying it intently. "An assignation with the morkani?"

"Oh damn." Holly hit the table with the flat of her hand. "When I think how *close* I was to finding out who it was . . ."

"It helps us not. Who's to say who owned the sigil? There is no way to prove it now."

Holly thought, The Old Town? "Well . . . who leaves the Hills?"

"Fletcher. On rare occasions, myself or the Master Sorcerer. But a traitor would not advertise; we look for someone who leaves secretly . . ."

"That's true."

They sat in companionable silence for a while, and after that talked inconsequentially while the afternoon darkened further. At last he stood.

"I'll bid farewell, Holly. I am called fool for going out of the Hills, but I'm not sorry I do."

"I'm glad you do." Holly pulled her slippers on and saw him to the door. "Hey—hang on a sec."

She dashed into the kitchen and reappeared with a jar of ground coffee. "Here, you have it. I can get some more. You just put boiling water on it—or milk, if you like it that way. I hope you get back OK."

He took the jar, put it in one of the coat's voluminous pockets, and clapped the battered hat on his head. "Thank you, Holly. Well, goodbye. I am glad, I think, that I'll not see you on the sands below Gallows Hill. That midnight will be no place for any human, no, nor elukoi either. Fare you well— and give my love to Fletcher."

16

Breaking Up

Mr Jones's fifth form were making the most of the last day of term. The time between the mid-morning break and the dinner hour was technically reserved for tidying classrooms; by custom it was the time of the class party.

"There 'e goes," observed Annette, another of Holly's friends. "Dear old Jonesy off to the staff-room for a cuppa. Won't see *him* again before dinner."

"Hooray!"

"That's not what you say!"

"Oh yes it is." Holly chuckled. "Er—did you get . . ."

"In a minute, in a minute. I gotta help Jenny with the stereo. 'Ang on."

Holly was sitting in Hut Five with Dodo Ogden. The classes circulated a lot at Christmas so it was not unusual to see a third former in a fifth form classroom.

The bare room had been decorated—if not smothered—in tinsel and crepe paper and hanging decorations. Within minutes it had acquired a party air; the chairs and desks were pushed back to the walls, a stereo record-player was set up, and Annette brought out two twelve-can packs of pale ale.

"Hand that round!"

"Who's got the bloody mugs?"

"Here's mine—hey, go easy!"

"What about me? Ta."

"What're we gonna have on?"

Holly retrieved her plastic beaker. She didn't ordinarily care for canned beer, but having some where it was forbidden was another matter. "What've you got?"

"Starren's Bethlehem Star—''

"Put Bethlehem Star on, we can dance to that," Jenny suggested.

"Why not?" Annette looked over their heads to the door. "Hey, somebody keep an eye open, just in case. I can have these cans outta sight in seconds."

"Aw, Jonesy won't mind."

"Sure. All we gotta do is offer him a drink!"

"Strychnine?" suggested a chorus of voices.

Holly joined the dancing, but retired breathless after a few tracks. She went to sit by the window, precariously balanced on a stack of chairs. Looking out she saw the wind had dropped slightly; thin powdery snow was being whisked over the ground and plastered against the buildings.

"Snow already?" Dodo appeared at her elbow, mug in hand.

"It won't lay, I bet." Holly was morose. "It's been ages since we actually had snow at Christmas."

"Yeah. Hey, you remember the year it started snowing Boxing Day and carried on clear through to March?"

"April," Holly contradicted. "It was snowin' on my birthday, and that's April four."

"Mine's always filthy. I didn't *ask* to be born in February! Wasn't it about that time it snowed so hard they sent us home at midday and we walked up through the Park?"

"Yeah, I remember that."

"There was you, me, Annette, Heather—who else?—oh yeah, Chris an' Diane."

"So there was." Holly thought: That's right, it was before me an' Diane had that row. Now she's over there with Gabriel, tellin' dirty stories by the sound of it. Damn her. An' Chris, over there with Carol—who does she think she's kidding? She's jittery as hell.

"She's been a bit weird this last term." Dodo glanced over at Chris. "Did you know, she quit going to Youth Club? And she never went in the table-tennis tournament, nor the ladies' football. I suppose you and her are still . . ."

"Yes."

"Don't you think you might—I mean, it is Christmas—"

"It's nothing to do with me," Holly snapped, envying Dodo her easy friendships.

"OK, OK." Dodo hastily changed the subject. "I was up the Hollington stables again las' night."

"Your dad still doing work there?"

"No. It's the Wrecker—"

"Who?"

"Whitefire."

"Oh, Strawberry's foal."

"That's him. Only everyone calls him the Wrecker now, he's so wild. Vicious. At least, he is with them, not me. I have to go up and feed him most nights, he won't let anyone else near him." She finished her drink. "It's a rotten shame, him being born like that."

"She had a rough time with him; I remember she was down in the field below us at the time."

"Yeah, but I mean . . . split hooves, and that deformed head. It's not fair. And he's OK really."

Yeah, kick your head in for tuppence! Holly thought. "Is he still growing?"

"Oh, yeah. He isn't six months old yet, and he's big as a yearling already. Me dad says he's a freak. That's why he's got all that wrong with him. He says freaks don't live long."

"The owner might not keep him, anyway."

"I would. If they'd let me. He knows me. But they might have to move him soon, isolate him. He disturbs the other horses."

"You're lucky, knowing that sort of people. I wouldn't mind a bit of horse-riding."

"You ought to come over one Saturday in the holidays, and bring that boyfriend of yours."

"Fletcher?" Holly queried. She had spent much time down in the stable-hut, but reading lessons were hardly romantic, she thought, especially when she had little patience and he had a frayed temper.

"Yeah, Fletch. You got another fella hidden away someplace? No, seriously; he's got a thing about animals, right?"

"Well, I guess—"

"I mean he never passes one but he talks to it; cat, dog, anything. And I mean *talk*."

"People do talk to animals."

"Not like they were people, they don't." There was a shrewd and suspicious look on the younger girl's face, that faded to remembered wonder.

"I saw him once, when he didn't think anyone else was there but him. Going home from the garage. There were crows in that field at the back, six or seven of them. He stopped and called to them. And they *came* to him. Perched on his arms."

Holly could see that as clearly as Dodo; the boy's arms stretched and swaying under the burden of black-feathered bodies. I didn't know, she thought, obscurely let-down, that he was so lonely. And Dodo? I was right at midsummer, sooner or later someone'll have to tell her; if only to warn her to keep off. But not yet; it can't be now, not yet . . .

The door clicked open; all conversation ceased. They stood like statues; only the music still pouring into the emptiness . . .

A small pigtailed third-year put her head round the door. " 'Scuse me—is Dodo Ogden in here?"

"Here, Heather."

"Sod off, both of you!"

"Move!" Annette made a threatening gesture and the two girls ran giggling up the passage. "Christ Jesus, I'm gonna have a heart attack if that happens again!"

"Aw, quit worryin'!"

Holly went back to the window. The snow was coming down in earnest now, the town being blotted out in grey veils. She was suddenly lonely; feeling as if she were standing outside the window where the light made a yellow square on the snow, looking in at the girls who danced and talked, hearing their chatter and music . . . out in the grey morning . . . alone . . .

Don't know why I'm miserable, she thought. Maybe it's just the tail-end of the cold. Or that this is the last Christmas party I'll have here. All the same, I wish next Sunday was over. I wish I never heard of midwinter.

"Bitch!"

Holly swung round, hearing Chris's voice sharp with anger. She was with Helen Gabriel and Diane Cooper.

"Screw you!" The black-haired girl had a half-full beaker in her hand; she threw the liquid in the shorter girl's face. Chris slapped the cup out of her hand and flew at her.

Violence was electric in the room. Girls scattered out of the way, snatching drinks and records to safety; then formed a shouting circle round the fighters.

"You pissin' cow!"

"Hold her, Hel! Get her!"

Not now! Holly thought. For Christ's sake, Chris, not *now*! It's practically dinner-time, Jonesy'll be back any second!

"Break it up!" Annette tried to separate them and caught a fist in the ribs that sent her staggering back.

"You sod!"

As Diane moved in Holly grabbed her arm and spun her away.

"Don't you touch her, Cooper! Leave 'em alone!"

"I'll get you—"

The desks came down with a floor-shaking crash. Chris and Helen lay dazed in a pile of beer cans, chairs, desks, broken glass, and satchels. In the utter silence that followed Holly heard footsteps in the passage outside.

"Christ, it's Taf Jones."

It was; and he had the headmistress with him.

"Stand away from them, you girls."

They backed away. Holly couldn't see properly, but she could hear one of the two girls crying—Chris, she thought.

"Who's hurt?"

Annette's voice was low. "My God, there's blood."

The headmistress took over. "Now then, you: Christine Ivy—where are you hurt?"

An indistinct mumble.

"Your arm? Yes, I see; that's a nasty cut. You'd better go down to sick bay and let Mrs McKay have a look at it. Who'll take her over to the main building?"

"I will, Mrs Mortimer."

"Good, Holly. Tell Mrs McKay Christine can use the sick-bed this afternoon if necessary."

Finding Chris on her feet Holly ushered her out of the room. As she shut the door she heard the headmistress ne change from kindly concern to flint.

"I mean to find out who is responsible for this. Helen Gabriel—"

"How'd you do your arm in?" Chris was trying to twist a handkerchief round it left-handed, and not succeeding; Holly took over.

"It's funny. The one thing Gabriel's goin' to get blamed for and she didn't do it. There's a sharp edge on one of those desk-hinges, it cut me coming down." Keyed up, she laughed on a note not far removed from hysteria. "All that booze —let's see the archangel Gabriel talk herself out of *that!*"

"OK, OK, go easy. Where's your coat? You'll need it going over to the main building, it's snowing."

"You leave me alone, Anderson. I don't need any help from you! I didn't get any either, did I? Oh, I forgot. You don't believe in fighting. You yellow bitch."

"I kept Cooper off your back; you'd've had two of 'em to deal with if it hadn't been for me—"

"Oh, piss off! You make me puke."

Holly didn't hold her back. She stood in the open door, watching until the blonde girl had reached the main building. She stood there for a long time, not looking at or thinking of anything. At last she went back in; only to meet Mrs Mortimer coming out.

"Ah, Holly, back already. Good. You can come to my office and tell me what you saw of this disgraceful incident. Mr Jones, kindly send the other girls along after dinner."

"I'll get you, Anderson," Gabriel promised as she went past. "An' you can tell your les friend that goes for her too. We'll be waiting for you."

The sun was a pale morning disc low in the south-east, gleaming on snow pocked only by lines of birds' tracks. Holly wandered by the pond's edge in the Park. Ducks waddled on the ice. The pine trees were bowed low and every few seconds a gob of snow would fall to the path beneath; white on white.

Church bells? Holly had been hearing them for some time, but only noticed it now. It is Saturday, not Sunday? Of course. I guess they must be practising. Monotonous.

The muffled slow tolling continued. She tried to place the church, but had to give it up as a bad job. By one bench she stopped.

That's where me an' Chris met Elathan ... She scooped snow from the wood, absently making snowballs; cold, but burning her bare skin like fire. That's a long time back now. Why the hell did we have to be smart? Why didn't we just give the damn coin back to Fletch? Hell!

She flung the snowball with sudden violence; watched it curve and fall and star the pond's ice.

"Hello."

As usual she hadn't heard him come. His Saturday off for Christmas, she remembered. "Cheers, Fletch."

He leaned on the rail beside her. Denims, heavy cord jacket; he was nothing but human. Although scrubbed, his hands were still grimy, the nails black with grease. "Hear that row in the field this morning? Scared me white; thought they were on to me."

"It's only the Wrecker." It had woken Holly at six, much to her disgust. "They're isolating him in that stable. Sorry I didn't warn you. Dodo said something about it to me, but like an idiot I didn't see it. Lucky they didn't bust in on you."

"Heard them coming. Anyway, my stuff's packed and out of the way, up in the loft."

Holly studied him, glancing sideways. Obviously he had something on his mind. She thought he'd changed since she first saw him. Taller, bony—he'd lost flesh lately—skin paler. Dark hair close to shoulder-length. Lines round the wide mouth that smiled less and less often.

Now why should I worry about him? she asked herself deprecatingly. Especially when I know I can't help him— I know what's on his mind—tonight; the elukoi—can't do a thing about that. Maybe Mathurin was right. We should've gone away.

Fletcher said, "I'm going back."

17

Snow in December

It was too abrupt. Holly was colder than the snow. She could not pretend to misunderstand him.

"To the Hills, tonight? Fletcher, what do you think you can *do*?"

"I don't know, probably very little. Still, I can handle a bow. I have to go back, to at least try to help. I can't leave them."

"You're nothing to do with them! They're not even—"

"—human? I thought you knew better than to say that."

"I do, I do. I didn't mean it like that. You know what I mean. You've got your own life. It's stupid to—well, to take risks where there isn't any need."

He was serious. "If they're fighting I have to be there. Sometimes you have to fight for what you think's right. Anyway, archers rarely get hurt if only one side has 'em. I'll stay a bow-shot away an' pick 'em off."

"Yeah, pick 'em off, shoot, kill! You don't even know what it means, you're just playing, being melodramatic. Silly goddamn schoolboy games! You don't know!"

"Don't I?"

"No!"

They were facing each other like enemies, breath clouding the crystal air. Fletcher glared at her—a grey-eyed girl, flushed with anger, glittering with fury. So sure of herself. Then he turned away, going to clear the bench of snow and slump down on it.

"All right then—" it was a boy's voice, choking "—all right, you tell me how I can stay here? Don't you see? He's my father. They're my friends. I'm not human; inside, where it matters, I'm elukoi! I don't remember being human, I've lived in the Hills all my life. Even if it's only for tonight, I've got to go. I can't let them down. Can't. Oh Christ."

His head dipped; his hands covered his face but only for a second. When he looked up he was shaking. He said quietly, "I thought you'd understand."

Holly had leant back against the pond-rail, gripping it tightly. Her palms were frozen; mottled blue and purple.

"Understand?"

Inside her head she had a collection of mental pictures of Fletcher, from the bright sunlight of Highrock to the feel of his arm light across her shoulders at the autumn fair. Now there was another, a boy in the snow, and she thought suddenly this might be the last.

She thought, He's right. You can't let people down. If he asks me, I'll go.

" I do understand. Look, Fletch—"

He interrupted: "Never mind. I know all your arguments. They're very good. Very logical." He had learned enough of human ways to be angry that she had seen him show emotion. "Except I can't be logical when my friends are in trouble. It must be very convenient for you, that logic."

"Convenient, is it?"

"It must keep you out of a good many fights."

"You—! I didn't know you thought that about me."

"Thought what?"

"That I'm a coward."

"Did I say that? I didn't say that. You must have a guilty conscience."

"Guilty conscience!"

"Well, you said it, I didn't."

"For someone brought up in a village of savages you learn human arguments very quickly."

"They are not savages!"

"True. True. You can civilise savages."

"You're a liar as well as a coward."

It was as if he'd struck her. A white flame of anger blossomed. Her hands clenched to fists.

"If that's all you've got to say there's no point in me carrying on with this conversation. Excuse me."

"That's right. Run away. You do a lot of it, don't you? But you can't keep running forever."

"You go to hell!" She walked away quickly, snow clogging her feet, leaving him standing under the trees. Almost ran. Turned round to shout, throat hoarse: "To hell! You can go to bloody *hell*!"

Her voice rang flatly in the snow. He did not answer. She ran on through the Park.

It had clouded over, Holly couldn't see what time the sun set. By two, it was pitch dark. By six, when she came home, she was being driven crazy by the church bell. She mentioned it to her mother.

"Bell, dear? I can't say I can hear a bell but then your young ears are sharper than mine. I know it's very oppressive today. I've had a headache since I woke up."

"Me too." Sharp ears? was her mental query. You couldn't miss it unless you were stone deaf. Bloody mournful thing; clang ... clang ... clang ... you'd think it was a funeral. And she can't hear it?

She realised then; as easily as if she'd known it all along. The sea-bells of Ys. The challenge for midnight, tonight, on the beach.

"I had a phone call from Ted Malory," her mother continued. "I expected you'd have been into the gallery to see him?"

Holly shook her head, only half listening, She had spent hours just wandering round the town centre. It had been a dark day, the sun low in the south; a few cars creasing lines in the slush, tyres hissing. She had had no heart for the windows full of bright lights and colours; Christmas trees, Christmas carols, Santa Claus, cribs—not even the Christmas pop music. Every roof and ledge had an icing of snow, rounding the harsh edges and making the town look clean; she had let the slow cold numb her body and her mind, not wanting to think.

"I never went along that way. What'd he want?"

"He says he's sold that painting of yours—the one of the apple tree. To a friend of his from Manchester. He says you can look in and collect your money any time—less his percentage."

"That's Ted Malory, OK!" Holly laughed for the first time that day. "Sold it, has he? *Jesus*—oh, sorry, Mum. But think— somebody liked it enough to pay money for it!"

Her mother laughed, echoing her pleasure. "You'd better get painting, I can always do with extra housekeeping."

"You'll be lucky!" She raced to the arctic regions of her bedroom, anxious to see if she had anything else that might be saleable

She drew the curtains and shut out the ghost-white world under its cold street lamps. It gave an illusion of cosiness, though her breath smoked in the air. She heaved an armful of paper and board canvases on to the bed.

My God, what rubbish. It'll have to go. I just haven't

got room. She hugged herself. There was a wild triumph burning under her ribs, she wanted very much to shout, and to dance. But then she stopped, sobered, and picked up one sheaf of papers fallen from a folder.

They were pencil sketches, and not very good. Silverleaf from the back; a waterfall of hair and a wild-animal stance. Brancaer from a distance; and the interior of the Great Hall. One of Elathan, torn through. Three of the Harper; one in firelight with the Harp, one head-and-shoulders from memory, and one three-quarter profile she had doodled absently on that winter afternoon when he called.

There were dozens of Fletcher; sitting, standing, leaning, bending over his books. Most she had done from memory, she had never dared ask him to sit for her; but some (the best) she had done while teaching him his letters down in the stable-shed.

Suddenly restless, she went back down into the sitting-room and turned the television up. Ys. Drowned Caer Ys. The bells of Ys, swinging slow and deep in fathom on fathom of icy sea; drowned in magic so deep they came to no human ears—except those who, by their nature, are spell-breakers.

'Popchart' was on; all the special Christmas recordings of Davy Starren, corn-blond, unspeakably arrogant; the rest of the group well in the background while he came on hot and heavy with 'Bethlehem Star'. Holly couldn't see him—only his uncanny resemblance to Fletcher.

He doesn't care, she thought, self-pityingly. He doesn't care at all. He's never said. Not a word. Doesn't know how I feel . . .

She looked up, caught her own woebegone expression in the mirror—and suddenly grinned.

My God, girl, you're ridiculous. How should he know? You've never said anything to him. It was all in your own head. She admitted to herself what she had known for a long time: I'll go. Try and get through it; hope nothing happens to any of us. But I can't just stand by and do nothing.

The rending crash of wood woke her. She shot to the window. There was a dark jagged hole where the door to Wrecker's stable had been. She picked up the clock.

Eleven forty-five p.m.

The alarm knob was down; she had silenced it in her sleep as she often did. The last bus to cross the marshes had gone long ago. Her eyes stung, but she had no time to cry over lost opportunities.

All right, I'll walk if I have to! She reached for her jeans, but another crash brought her back to the window.

The doors of Fletcher's shed were beaten in. Snow flurried down the field, out of sight.

Fletcher! (Heart in mouth.) Has he gone yet? The elukoi move fast, he might not go till the last minute—is he down there, hurt?

She dressed hurriedly, thinking, I'll be late anyway. I must just check first, and find out if he's gone. Oh damn that bloody Wrecker!

More snow had fallen, it was over her ankles. She pushed through the thin hedge into the field, wiping the wet snow from her face and neck. Flying hooves scattered a blizzard. The Wrecker was down the field, then, and beyond her view.

The moon had risen full. She saw plainly by its light, and picked her way to the shed and peered in.

Place is tidy, stuff's gone. Yes . . . so's he, obviously. Thank the Lord for that.

A ringing neigh. She swung round. The Wrecker bulleted across the bottom of the field, snaking from shadow to shadow.

That horse is wild! I'd better shift. She could see no light in any house in Stonegate Street, including her own. I've wasted enough time. I've got to go while I can.

Ragged grey clouds patched the sky. The stars burned brighter. A chill wind brought sounds of geese calling in the Park and a train far down in the town station. Numb with cold, Holly felt herself wide awake in nightmare.

Up the track to the road, she decided. From there I can walk to Hallows Hill, via the Junction. Then down to the sea road. It's gonna take best part of an hour. If I can get out of here without that horse seeing me ...

The snow dragged at her feet. They hurt with the cold. Half running, half walking, she made for the gate.

Bright moonlight. Too bright! A thunder of hooves and a horse-scream and Holly panicked. She threw herself towards the gate as the Wrecker came up behind her.

Nothing should move that fast! Then her leg twisted, she came crashing stunned and brittle to earth, and the razor-sharp hooves came flailing down ...

18

Midwinter

Nothing hurt.

Holly couldn't believe it. She uncurled, flat on her back in the wet snow, and opened her eyes.

To either side, a hoof; cloven and swathed in white hair like a shire-horse's. The Wrecker straddled her. Looking up she saw, not the bared teeth of a vicious horse, but a single jutting horn.

She was cold—and recognised it. At midsummer she had heard a name and felt this same biting coldness, and the name had been—Fyraire, Lord of Stars.

The horn was spiralled, sword-straight and sharp, and it hovered by her throat. On her face was the warm animal breath of the Unicorn; and the night stars were blotted out by the beast towering over her. It fell into place in a second: Strawberry's foal, born midsummer day, the day the Harp of Math called him.

"Fyraire!"

He reared up and back, horn raking the darkness; hooves thudding into the slush. Holly caught her breath—he shone like the moon. She lifted herself on her elbows, not caring for the moment if he trampled her or not, so long as she could look.

He quieted; lowered his head and sniffed at her.

Inside her head was a sudden burning and flowering of

images; darkness, silver, cold, and an awesome immensity, intolerably bright. It became less intense; her mind could not hold it. She realised then that it came from him; and because she could not comprehend him, she was translating that full flood into a tiny trickle of words.

You call me by name, and you have a smell of magic about you . . . where are my people? I have come the only way open to me to find them, but I do not know this land.

Aware that she was wet and cold, Holly sat up and pulled her legs under her, and got unsteadily to her feet. It all fitted. Dodo's Wrecker, sick, deformed, split-hooved, misshapen in head and body—or the Unicorn, cloven-hooved, newly horned, not a horse at all, thicker at the shoulder, leaner hipped, and more noble of carriage than any equine beast. Mane and tail whipped about him; a storm of light.

"I'd better go. Magic has no effect on me; I break spells. You might get hurt. . . ." It sounded absurd when she said it.

He came closer, his breath warm and cloudy in the frosty night. *I am real. Here or in Faerie, I am real. Lord of Stars, Master of Tongues; above magic and science both. Yet I am lost . . . human, where are my people? You have been with them, I read signs of that.*

"The elukoi—" she stopped. This was the Unicorn, Mathurin had called him. But what had he called? Nothing that could be controlled. Hooves like razors, and a murderous horn; and brilliant pictures in her head . . .

She thought, Chris stops magic but she couldn't stop him. Nobody could.

"I'm not going to tell you where the elukoi are until you tell me why you want them." She backed up a step without meaning to, feeling small and defenceless. He dipped his head and looked directly into her eyes. His were a gold-flecked sea-green, mesmeric, and faintly humorous.

Listen, human. I was called here by the Harp and I came; but for what I do not know. Only those of Faerie could play Math's Harp so. But elu-k'oi . . . in their tongue that is beast-friend. Who are they?

"You don't know?"

I came here the only way I could, born mortal, for the Silver Wood was closed to me then. It is not an hour since that I became myself and knew that I was Fyraire. Of this world I know naught since the fall of Caer Ys.

"Jesus Christ . . . !" Absently Holly brushed caked snow from her. "I'll have to tell you. I trust you."

She told him as quickly as she could: South Street and Orionë and the Hills. She felt his mind moving with hers, was sure at the end that he knew all that she did.

"Now what?" she said.

Find them.

"And then?"

The horn rested for a moment on her shoulder, reassuring her. She forgot the cold that shivered through her and froze hands and feet; forgot the iron-bitter wind.

Courage. If anything is to be salvaged from this sorry mess, we are the ones to do it. Time is wasting.

"They're on the beach, over the Gallows Hill side of the marsh."

Where is that?

The realisation hit her hard. He doesn't know, and it's too complicated for me to explain—

You must show me. Come. I will carry you.

She opened her mouth, shut it again, not sure that she had taken his meaning. He couldn't mean . . . "Ride you?"

You will not be riding me, you have not the look of a rider—I will be carrying you. You will be safe. Now, hurry! Which way?

"West almost all the way, then south."

She reached up and put her arms over his white shaggy back, heaved herself up, threw one leg over his rump and was sitting high and steady and amazed.

Hold on!

My God! Holly grabbed two fistfuls of flying mane and clung on. Churned snow flew past her, black shadows swallowed them in and spat them out into bright moonlight again. The Unicorn galloped for the gate, gathering himself together like a steel spring, and soared clear over it. One stride; over the Park fence into a private field, racing west like a sea-gale. Holly clung to his back, feeling the powerful muscles bunching and the drumming of the hooves beating down the earth. Cold air whipped hair into her eyes and mouth, her wet clothes were clinging to her; but she held on, shouting wordless encouragement until her mouth was dry.

They cleared another fence effortlessly, scattered plants throughout a row of gardens, and clattered out on to the tarmac of Birchdale Junction. Street lamps shut them in under a tent of white light; traffic lights gleamed red, red-amber, green.

Fyraire checked. *Which way?*

"There—the second one—" Holly picked the Combe Marish road, the route unrolling in her head. He didn't need roads. Take it cross-country, direct, go up the back of Hallows Hill—

He exploded into movement again. Hooves rang on the slushy road. They wheeled into the Combe Marish turning, and were suddenly blinded by headlights. Holly felt her throat sore with a scream. The powerful body under her surged up and forward—she glimpsed a white blurred face behind the windscreen—heard his hooves spang off metal, clipping the roof—they were gone into the night.

"Faster!" *They'll never explain that one, never!* She shook, nearly lost her grip, half-hysterical.

They swung right, cleared a low garden fence, scattered gravel, another fence; and they were in the long field sloping down to the railway line at the back of Hallows Hill.

She had thought him fast before, but now he could see a clear way he stretched out into a full gallop. The white world floated past in moonlight. She had to put her head down on the Unicorn's neck to be out of the wind and to breathe.

How far now?

"Up the hill, under the railway bridge. Round the edge of the marshes. The beach."

A ring on metal; a scatter of gravel; the railway line. He did not pause or slow going up the hill. They came out under the bridge, and in front of them the marshes lay pallid under snow.

They halted. Holly sat up, aching. It was here that she and Chris had met Fletcher one summer morning, before they knew anything of the Hills. The Hills' entrance was drowned in mist that stretched westward, hiding Gallows Hill and Combe Marish. Sea mist? Holly frowned. *Can't see anything. No knowing if they're fighting on the beach—but it's a fair bet they are. Don't let anything happen to them!*

"Stay on this side of the hill—you can get down round the marsh to the sea road."

Her head ached from the mental pressure; and she still found herself, if she wasn't careful, looking at things with his vision—brighter and stranger and splendid.

A storm of snow went up behind them. The shoulder of the hill loomed on the left in black shadow. They burst into clear light again and swung west on the little road; six inches deep in snow and no tyre tracks. Holly saw little of it, hunched forward and trying to snatch air. Pebbles flew past her face, she realised they were on the beach. The moonlight dimmed and was gone. They entered the bank of sea fog and the hard-packed sand echoed to their passing.

Holly heard the elukoi and morkani before she saw them: a great shout of alarm and terror as Fyraire came down on them. She tightened her fists in his mane and peered over his shoulder. In this mist she could just make out a crowd separating—one group fled towards the marshes, the other to the sea.

We made it—but what's he going to do?

Fyraire was on them like a lightning bolt, his speed driving them apart like a spear splitting wood. They ran. Elukoi and morkani both, they ran in panic, and what had been two armies became a demoralised mob. The Unicorn checked, wheeled—

Holly lost her grip and fell and hit the ground hard, the wind knocked out of her, stinging all over; feeling she might shatter into small pieces if she moved. The night was full of shouting and the drumming of hooves. Shrill and angry the Unicorn bugled his challenge across the beach, and they fled before him. But Holly could make out from where she lay that, though he beat the two sides apart, he hurt neither; the pearl-silver horn was unstained.

She had fallen by a knot of people who were not running but standing, as if thunderstruck. Two broke away, coming towards her; then there was a hand under each arm, hauling her upright.

"Talk about an ace in the hole!" Chris was jubilant, pounding her back. "How'd you swing that one, girl?"

"Are you all right?" Fletcher, bow over his shoulder.

"I'm OK—Christ, I ache!" She clutched her ribs; then her legs, that seemed to have gone to water at the joints.

She hung on to Chris as they rejoined the group. Oberon stood remote, his eyes on small huddled darknesses on the sand. Bodies, Holly realised, staring with horrified fascination through the mist. There were few, and she could see no details.

Elathan and Mathurin were there, and Eilunieth, girt with a sword; and two more at a distance. They were morkani, dark-haired, in shining mail; a man and a woman. As Holly came closer she recognised the woman's face.

I saw that on the Hawk-sigil! And the tapestries in Orionë. —no, this is younger. Tanaquil's daughter, Tanaquil Seahawk.

They had the same expression on their faces—sheer surprise, and something else; remembrance and wonder and hunger. The morkani woman tore her gaze from the Unicorn and swung round angrily:

"You told me the Harp was broken! You swore the summoning had failed!"

"Tanaquil, I tried!"

Holly knew that desperate voice, but she refused to accept what his reply meant.

"Harper?" Elathan stared at him disbelievingly. His hand dropped to his sword but Eilunieth stopped him, the same shock showing on her face.

"Stop. It is not for you to judge."

"I thought—anybody. But not him. Not him." Fletcher's voice was no more than a whisper, he did not take his eyes from the Harper. "All the time trusting him, and he was doing that to us."

Holly thought, I don't believe it. But he's not denying it. Oh I wish it had been anybody but him, I liked him.

The Harper was quiet, not defending himself. He turned away as the Unicorn's call rang out again, but this time not in anger, and watched Fyraire come cantering through the mist to them. The elukoi and morkani began to draw together again, but with no thought of battle, forming a ring round the Starlord and their leaders. Torches were lit. Holly saw Sandys carrying one—he bore no weapon, but a healer's satchel of herbs—and Silverleaf also; she carried a longbow.

The sea-people were beautiful.

Holly stared at them, great numbers gathering, most of the crowd hidden by the fog. She had expected monsters. Seeing them she knew them for people of Faerie, even though their ages under the sea had changed them. Gleamingly pearl-skinned where the elukoi were tanned brown, hair shading from Tanaquil's emerald green to Fiorin's blue-black instead of red and gold; prick-eared and slim and tall and strong —part of Faerie, despite web-fingers, and beautiful.

Their eyes gleamed gold.

People of Faerie, do you know me?

A muttering; a whisper from mouth to mouth: yes. Holly knew they heard as she did; a bell-voice that was no voice, but images behind the eyes.

Fyraire's horn glanced on Oberon's shoulder, and he stood taller, and they embraced.

"We thought you'd not come, Lord."

I was called. Who called me?

"I did," Mathurin answered, and met the Unicorn's green-gold eyes.

You are not Math, but you have the look of him.

"I am his son."

Down the beach the sea roared blackly. The tide was turning, coming in. Holly huddled into her anorak.

We have little enough time. People of the House of the Hawk, it is long and long that you have been in bondage to the Mother of Bitter Waters. Say: shall that be ended?

"We have served Rak-Domnu since the days of my mother." Tanaquil glanced nervously at Fiorin. "You were but a legend, Lord of Stars. Yet do I now renounce and utterly abhor the Mother of the Abyss and all her works. I will speak the truth: it has been weary, that bondage."

Fiorin's face twisted bitterly. Holly saw he had a knife in his hand, dull-coloured, flint. He said, "Will you betray us all, and Her too?"

"Fiorin, be silent. Even you cannot say we should give battle now; it is sure we cannot defeat the elukoi with the Lord of Stars fighting on their side."

I am not on the elukoi side.

"What?" Elathan barked.

"Still; I will not fight, even though that be true. I have worked against this war for a long time now—I and one other."

The look she gave Mathurin was unmistakable. Holly couldn't say she liked Tanaquil, but she thought the woman had courage. She was beginning to be scared again—that Fyraire might be on the side of the sea-people was something she had never considered.

"You have the soul of a whore and a traitress. Starlord, if you are with us—"

I am not for the morkani, Fiorin of the Bitter Waters.

"Then who?"

I am for the people of Faerie.

That took a moment to sink in, but Holly saw Mathurin's face light up and realised what he had seen—no more fighting. Chris dug her in the ribs; and she heard Fletcher's fierce whisper: "Good!"

"Then there is not to be a battle?"

There is not.

The Harper broke in: "There is more, is there not? The stars be right; as they were uncounted years ago when we asked of you that you lead us here. Lord, an we should ask now that you open the way back to Faerie, what say you to that?"

I say: who asks me? It is a difficult road back. I tell you this for certain sure, either all go, or none at all ... There is little magic left in you, sea-people, hill-dwellers; you are each too weak alone. I say, come now before it is too late. There is no room for magic in this world any longer; they will hunt you down and drive you out. Come back now.

Elathan could scarcely speak for anger. "If you only knew all that they have done—!"

"We?" Fiorin spat. "You stealers of children, you roll in the muck with the rest of the beasts—"

"Murderers!"

"Animals!"

"It has gone on too long." Eilunieth, weary. "You see, Lord? Too long and too bitter have we waged this war. There is hatred between us."

"Listen—"

Elathan turned on the Harper. "Be silent!"

"I will not be silent! This is not your decision. And I crave your pardon, my Lord Oberon, my Lady Eilunieth; but it is not for you to say, either."

The crowd hemmed them in. The Harper faced away from the Starlord, in the island of torchlight. Beyond that circle the fog and the dark closed in. He spoke to the hundreds who waited. Holly saw that he too was unarmed.

"It is not for Oberon or Elathan or Tanaquil or Fiorin to say to you, you will do this or you will do that. That is the way of mortal men—and we be of Faerie. All of us, elukoi and morkani both; we are of Faerie, we, who of old were great.... You know now that the Lady Tanaquil and I have striven against this fighting for a long time. I have done things it may be were ill done, but I did them in the belief that we are one people. It is for you to prove me liar, or not.

"But I speak not to hill-dweller or sea-born now, I speak to each of you alone. As with you, I was born in this world, I have never seen Faerie. But I want it, I ache for it; it is born in our blood that we want it—is it so with you?"

"Yes!" This from Silverleaf, and a few other scattered voices.

"So I speak to each of you alone. Stay if you wish; fight civil and bloody war as puppets of the Abyss; and—yes—one side will win. Which? I know not, and I care not. It will be such a hollow victory as was never seen before between here and the High Stars! Do you know why?

"I will tell you. We are the immortals—but not here! We are the undying—but only in Faerie, not on Earth! Whoever wins this battle, loses; because when they have won there is nothing for them to do but stay here, grow old, and die!"

He's getting to them, Holly thought. Now, Harper—finish it!

"We have fought each other, we have killed. Whose fault is that? I say we do not know and it does not matter! It was too long ago that this began to put the blame on any but one, and that one—is Rak-Domnu. There is grievous fault on both sides, elukoi and morkani, there is much to be forgiven. What the elukoi have done to the morkani is not more nor less than that which the morkani have done to the elukoi. I say: let it all be forgot! We may start again. We can go home."

"Aye, aye; forget, you say—forget what murder has been done! My wife, my friend—"

"My sister," Tanaquil put in softly, "Master Elathan, sea-people have died too."

Now must I warn you—the Unicorn, urgent—*we are close*

*enough here for Domnu to reach us. If you abandon her, Seahawk,
she will fight. We stand in danger.*

The Harper glanced seaward, nodded, and turned back
to the waiting crowd. He took Tanaquil's hand, and they
went to stand by the Unicorn.

"We are for the elukoi, the morkani, for the Lord of Stars
against Rak-Domnu. We are for freedom, for immortality,
and for Faerie; to free ourselves from the Abyss if we may,
and if not, to defy her as long as we can."

"Who is with us?"

19

Rak-Domnu

Silence; except for the sea's dull roar.

Come *on* . . . Holly held her breath, knowing then what Mathurin intended. They had come here to fight and he had cooled their hatred by putting Faerie into their heads; as bright and overwhelming as lightning. Immortality—the sweet reward held before them. Last, for those who still sought war, a common enemy—Domnu. It wouldn't work normally, but there's Fyraire—it must work!

"I forbid this!" Elathan cried in anguish.

"I am of the Harper's mind—it is not for you to say. Think you that we wish to grow old and die? Sorry, Master Elathan." Silverleaf walked without faltering to stand with Mathurin. Westwind followed, and after a pause, Hawk-hunter.

A stir. One of the morkani pushed to the front of the crowd. He was tall, olive-haired and greying at the temples; clad in silver fish-mail and carrying a flint-tipped pike. The torchlight sent his shadow monstrously across the churned snow and sand.

"I am with you. Immortality is strong bait."

"Brionis. I might have guessed. You were ever a coward, Brionis. Well, I'll not have even a coward desert me. Get back!"

"Not I. Fiorin."

"I command you—"

"Not any more, Priest of the Abyss. Not now and not ever again." He raised the pike and snapped the shaft over his knee, and threw the pieces at Fiorin's feet. "We will have what is ours by right!"

They took up the cry, and others with them, until Holly found herself standing deafened and cheering in the centre of a shouting swaying crowd; elukoi and morkani; and she knew that the Harper had won them over at last. And there were tears icy on her skin. The crowd called out for Mathurin and cried for Tanaquil, and they would not be silent until the Starlord paced slowly forward; and then the noise died down.

Holly stood on tiptoe, craning to see what was happening. They had drawn together about Fyraire and Oberon and Eilunieth. She thought, What about Elathan?

"Well, Master Sorcerer?" Mathurin's voice. He was out of her sight then.

"You fool. Do you think I have not known from the beginning that the sea-people were not our true enemies? There was only ever one—Domnu. We might have beaten the Seahawk's people, but never the Mother. Never! Her darkness and power is boundless. And now, within sight of her, on this night of all nights, you take her people from her." Elathan lifted his head. "But—I do not see how we might have moved events to avoid this. So for what it is worth, I am with you."

In the crowd Holly was pressed against Fletcher, and she felt him let out his breath in a deep sigh of relief.

Mist came up whiter and colder from the sea. The figures round her blurred—elukoi, morkani; foxes, stags, mares, stallions, hounds, falcons; the beasts who fought with the elukoi—Tanaquil with a gull hawk-wise on her wrist, Oberon with Tarac on his shoulder; Holdfast and Lightfoot with Silver-leaf . . . the rest was night and shadow and torchlight glittering on mail and blade and hair. She and Chris kept close together.

Fiorin spoke coldly. "You are determined on this, then, to withstand by force of arms whatsoever the Seamother may send against you? For I know that with these mortal children here there is a ban on such sorcery as you might employ."

Tanaquil answered for all. "We are so determined."

"Then you are witless! You do not know what power is in the Abyss. You do not know that even now you may not set foot off this beach—and the sea is coming, mark me well, the sea is coming!"

"And you, Fiorin, will you not come with us while there is time? Take heed for yourself; we are enough for the return to Faerie, I do not think one more or less will make a difference."

Fiorin spat at the Seahawk's feet.

"I curse you!"

He flung both arms up before him. Holly shrank back but the press of bodies was too great. The sea-born's glittering eyes were inhuman.

"I curse you all in Domnu's name! I curse you sleeping or waking, loving or hating, fighting or at peace, living or dead. I curse you, mortal or immortal, on land or on sea—"

Brionis shouted, "Join us or go!"

"—and I summon up against you the power of Rak-Domnu, I, Fiorin, Priest of the Bitter Sea; I call into myself the power of the Abyss—"

He stopped, covered his face, then let his hands fall limply. His head lifted. Holly heard the sharp intake of breath all round her; her stomach turned over.

Chris whispered, "If that's an act it's too bloody good."

He spoke again:

"Do you know me? House of the Hawk, do you know me?"

The Lord of Stars paced forward but the seaborn never moved. There was not a yard between him and that murderous horn.

I know you, Domnu.

"And I you, Lord of Beasts. Shall we finish what was begun in Caer Ys, think you?"

Chris was bewildered. "What's he at?"

"He called Domnu." Fletcher shuddered, "She's come."

There is nothing for you to fight for, Domnu. The House of the Hawk will not return to sunken Ys, they will not worship you again.

"But I will not let them go. I am the Sea, eternal. I have endured as long as this earth, and none may count the days of it; and when I die this world goes down in dust. I have swallowed down cities and towns and continents; mortals and beasts and gods; good men and evil men; kingdoms and empires. There is no end to the dead within me. The Abyss hungers, and all the blood in the world cannot satisfy it. You shall not leave this place."

The cold bit into Holly; numbed feet, hands and face; sunk into her bones. Domnu's words numbed her mind. She had become used to Ys's bell tolling in her head, but now it rang deeper and slower and louder. There was nothing in the world but cold and fog and the sea. She thought dumbly, I am drowning.

Fire!

Fierce white light: the Starlord rears up and cries defiance, and behind him they shake off that cold nightmare and raise weapons and make a great shout against Rak-Domnu!

Fiorin's face went slack. He pitched forward and fell

heavily, with no attempt to break the fall. The Unicorn
sniffed at him.

"Is he dead?"

*He lives, Seahawk, but I fear for his mind; it was not strong
enough to contain her. He may be imbecile if he survives.*

"We will care for him, an we live through this night. He
was once great, or ever we came to Ys." Two of the morkani
went at her signal to Fiorin's body.

"Indeed, if we live through this night . . . we should go
afore the Seamother attacks," Mathurin Harper advised.

Elathan nodded. "Nine of every ten morkani you have
won over with your words; the rest will hinder our going
if they may. Also there will be spells, like as not, so that
we should lose direction and find nought but sea every way
we go. Yet we have a remedy for that."

Come here.

Holly went with Chris and Fletcher to Fyraire.

You and you—he did not use their names, but Holly felt
her and Chris's images in his mind— *must go in midst of us.
First, that your protection extend over all; second, that we can
defend you.*

"But the marshes—" Elathan was struck by a sudden
thought, never having considered retreat. "To skirt them
gives Domnu too long a time to attack us. The direct path
we have not used these hundred years and more . . ."

"I found it. I know it." Fletcher, confident.

"Then find our way for us, boy. Now—go!"

Holly stood in the middle of that fighting force. Chris and
Mathurin were by her, but everyone else she knew had gone
ahead with Fletcher and Fyraire.

"Fear nothing. Keep walking, and nought shall harm."
The pressure of Mathurin's hand moved her forward. It was too

dark here, without the torches, to see what the others did around her.

"Who's afraid?" Holly thought, Who am I kidding?

Now there was a torch-bearer not far behind her. She could just see the mailed backs of morkani moving ahead of her. She was hemmed in. Whatever attacked, she wouldn't see it.

"Something's up." Chris was tall enough to see through the ranks to the head of the line, where there were a dozen spluttering torches. "We're stopping."

They stood for several minutes, stamping their feet against the cold. The column began to move slowly at last. Holly saw what lay ahead.

The sea.

Black and sullen, rolling past them to the west; the torches sending yellow flares across its oily darkness. Holly, tight with fear, thought, But we were supposed to be OK . . .

Silver came hunting down the line, spear in hand. She smiled as she passed them. "The tide comes in apace, we'll beat it an we hurry. It is no more than a handspan deep, but 'ware mud."

Holly remembered walking the beach in past summers and remembered the long shallow inlets that cut the sand off from the shingle when the tide came in. She was not afraid of that.

The mud sucked hungrily at her feet, but she came to dry land in half a dozen jerking steps. The ranks closed up again as they crunched up the long slope, going inland.

"Jesus, am I glad you turned up." Chris grinned. "Knew you wouldn't let me down, though. Even if you did leave it a bit late."

You've got a nerve. "It wasn't me. It was all him. Fyraire."

"Yeah." The blonde girl lost her smile. "He scares me. I mean, things like that shouldn't exist—they can't. The rest I can explain. But not him."

"He won't hurt you." The mist deadened their voices; along with the marching feet, and the clink of mail and sword and shield.

"That's not what I'm afraid of. It's just—there he is. And things like him didn't ought to be."

Shouts ahead. A twang and a hiss; Holly knew it for the sound of an arrow loosed. More of them—too many to count. The ground rising. A scramble over a bank, a flat stretch of snow, another bank—the road, she realised. Isolated shouts came from all sides now, but she could see nothing —not even Mathurin or Chris—now their one torch was gone.

"We're being attacked." Chris's voice, not where she expected it to be. "Reckon we're safe here."

"You hope."

The column thinned. In the marsh they could go no more than three abreast; the middle one keeping his hand on the shoulder of the one in front, while those to left and right defended themselves. Holly was flanked by two elukoi bowmen, and felt Mathurin's hand on her shoulder. The man in front was a tall morkani. She could not reach his shoulder and so clung to his swordbelt. The mud was over her ankles. The fog closed in. She could see nothing.

And her eyes kept shutting. The flu had given her a week of sleepless nights, and drained her body's resources badly. Neither cold nor the razor's edge of danger could keep her awake now. She gave a jaw-cracking yawn. The hand behind pushed forward. The belt yanked her sideways. She skidded and recovered. An arrow was loosed at her ear.

"Get him, Starkweather?"

"I think not—sea take that boy, he's led us astray, I swear. It was never so far to the Hills before."

I could get killed, she thought, dizzy with lack of sleep. It must be gone one o'clock. Again she stumbled. The ground was never where she expected it, and the mud betrayed her at every step.

More arrows, but all in silence. Holly knew she would break and run if anyone was hit and cried out.

Solid ground underfoot.

Holly rubbed her eyes; tried also to rub warmth into her frozen cheeks and chin and nose. The fog had cleared a little. She could see moon and stars in the roof of the sky. Also a dark ridge of ground: the gate to the Hills.

"Where's the rest?"

"Gone through. We've to go in last, keep Domnu from any magic—Holly!"

"What? Oh, sorry, Chris."

"For Christ's sake stay awake, girl."

Holly kept her eyes open, but time disjointed itself into sudden pictures. The Harper's face, intent in torchlight, peering out where mist hung like thick cotton wool, filigreed with the moon ... Fletcher with the longbow, arm going back smoothly, and the hissing shock of the arrow's flight ... Chris, hunched and cold ... shapes that moved but could not be clearly seen—

"They are all in, Harper."

"Go, then. At least Domnu cannot take the Hills while the Starlord holds the Gate."

Holly made no protest when the Harper bent down and scooped her like a child into his arms; she was asleep instantly. She had no memory of passing for the third time into the Hollow Hills.

Seaward, the bells of Ys fell silent.

Holly woke in bed with a sour taste in her mouth. Disappointment flooded in on her. *Dreamed it? I might've damn well known.*

She had never been so reluctant to face the morning. Stirring uneasily she rubbed at her gritty eyes, saw the blurred edge of a green pullover and silver watchstrap.... Pullover?

She rubbed her eyes until they watered, and her vision cleared. Two undyed wool blankets lay over her, and she could feel that she was fully dressed except for shoes and anorak. The bed was low and hard. Beside her, a hunched lump in the blankets, a spray of uncovered white hair— Silverleaf. Beyond her, Chris; on her back with her mouth open, one arm flung over the edge of the bed.

Holly slid out from under the covers and felt for her shoes. The brick floor was chilly. She moved to one of the scattered wool rugs. Shoes and anorak. She yawned, stretched, and went to the window. In the half-dark she gazed down on the top branches of a pine. Every needle was thickly encrusted with snow, making the tree resemble some stiff underwater sponge-growth. Other trees, elm and beech, spread out white fans of snow-laden twigs. The ground was lighter than the sky; but the last pre-dawn mists were dispersing and she saw a red glow beginning in the east.

Of course it's all true. She pushed her hair away from her face, wishing for a comb. She plaited it back roughly, finding an elastic band in her pocket. *I remember—the beach. Mathurin, Fiorin. And who else but me could fall asleep in the middle of a battle?*

The other two did not wake as she left. Once outside, the frosty air roused her. She strolled through an orchard, and came out on top of the eastward-facing slope of Brancaer's hill. The frozen meadow lay below her, and the still stream, and the silent forest. The sun was split by the tree-horizon; a deep red globe that shot the snow with pink and gold, crimsoned the dawn-mist, cleared the sky to winter brightness, and threw long blue shadows westward. Behind her the city was asleep.

She stretched again, shaking her head. Then she ran a few steps, kicked up sprays of snow, slipped, and rolled yards down the hill. Breathless she staggered back up the slope, swung on the trunk of a rowan till it stood crimson-berried and bereft of snow; then leaned against it, laughing weakly. They had come clear through it—herself and Chris and Fletcher, elukoi and morkani, and Fyraire of the Silver Wood! Her exultation demanded a physical outlet.

The sun cleared the horizon, went from red to gold, too bright now to gaze at. Holly heard a drum-beat sound from the north and twisted round to see what caused it. Far out across the open field three swans flew, low, but gaining height with every slow wingbeat. They swung in a rising curve towards her, long necks outstretched like geese, wings outspread. She felt them shake the air above her, a white thundercrack, and for a second saw the morning sun through stainless feathers.

They vanished into Brancaer. And she was quiet, and her joy ran deep.

The city was waking, the first spirals of smoke went skyward. The day was clear blue, clean, and bitter cold. One icicle hung from the rowan tree. Holly snapped it off and sucked it, still kneeling in the snow.

"You are awake early."

With animal carelessness, barefoot in the snow; bareheaded too, and with no weapon—Mathurin Harper.

"So're you."

"Will you walk with me? I would talk with you."

Holly nodded agreeably. She stood and dusted snow from her jeans and went with him down the hill.

20

The Last Morning

All the hazels and hawthorns were stiff with snow, and dead reeds jutted up from the ice at the fringes of the river. Away from the reed-javelins the water ran quick and black. Wisps of white vapour glided across it. Holly walked with Mathurin by that monochrome river, cutting deep swathes in the snow that was marked only by bird tracks.

"You're going, aren't you? All of you. When?"

"Now. As soon as they have all they wish to take with them. And none to blame them, girl, not even you." He looked up at the forest, casting its shadow down towards the stream. "Earth moulds them to her pattern; would give them children, take their immortality—given time, would make them as human as you . . ."

"I don't blame anyone—for anything." Holly was not sure if she meant to needle him or not.

"No, that is true." He dropped an arm loosely across her shoulders. "If you could only come with us, the marvels I could show you! But no mortals go to Faerie."

Holly grinned up at him, liking him still. As an only child, she had always wanted brothers. (She knew too many girls to have illusions about sisters.) Mathurin would have been a good elder brother, she thought.

"No wonder you knew so much about those sigils." She was jealous for a brief second. "I suppose Tanaquil gave it to you?"

He nodded. "We met and loved, and after the ancient custom of Faerie we exchanged tokens. To her I gave one of the silver harpstrings of Math's Harp. And to me she gave one of the royal seals of Ys."

"Bit careless with it, weren't you?" But she smiled to show she didn't mean it.

"That was ill-luck, to lose it out of the Hills, and in the human town—for I had to put blame on something, and chose a Well-coin for similarity; hoping I could get it back, and my folk not see it closely."

"You should've come for it."

"How could I, and I an elukoi? I had no choice but to send the boy, a human among humans."

"But you came to my house last autumn . . ." she stopped. She remembered the disguise he had used. And she remembered the man she had seen reflected in a glass window the day she found the coin. I knew it was him, she thought, I just never made the connection.

She frowned. "That night, after I found the coin . . ."

"I sent Scathlach." He cupped his hand to his shoulder. As in Orionë months ago, she saw a small grey animal there —a mouse. "He's not clever, but has a fondness for harper's music, and is an excellent small spy. But that time he failed, and came back in panic fear—do you maybe have a cat?"

"We've got a dog," Holly prevaricated, remembering that reality had seemed a dream.

They turned and began to trudge up the hill again towards Brancaer. Holly saw frantic activity, and realised how fast her last morning was passing.

"What about Orionë?" She wanted him to deny it. "Did you tell the morkani it was unguarded?"

"Listen, there was a choice. Elathan's way, to fight. My way, the summons—the which was no more than delay."

He saw her surprise. "I did not believe Fyraire would come. Or if he did, there be legends of him—dark and bloody and savage. He is wild. I thought if the caverns were destroyed, then also the Harp. Then no summoning, and no war either, for a time . . ."

Savage? Holly recalled the beach. Yes. When I think what he *might* have done.

Under Brancaer's trees, the sun made white hollow caves of the groves, and diamond lights of every icicle and pane of glass.

"I sent a message for all to come to the Council from the caverns, I wanted no elukoi hurt. Do you believe that?"

"You know me. I believe you."

"And when I thought Eilunieth was dead—"

"Every sword has two edges." It was Eilunieth, inhumanly impassive. She favoured one hip, as if that leg had not healed, and an ugly red scar puckered the left side of her face. With her was Tanaquil. One in blue, one in green with russet hair; they were bright against the snow as a stained-glass window.

Holly saw Tanaquil's face soften, meeting Mathurin's yellow eyes. Again she was jealous, but thought, He came to *me* to explain. I can remember that, when this is finished.

He said, "The rest you know."

"There was one thing you could've done—you knew Chris was gonna help at midwinter. If she hadn't, they might not have fought. You could've had something happen to her."

"But I did not. I could not."

"No," She was reassured. "I know."

Tanaquil's deep voice came in. "Many of us would have paid that price for peace, an we had known, but not he. Ah, those were bad times. Fiorin had the power of Domnu, and led us all. You do not know what that was like."

"*I* don't, at any rate." Holly asked, "What was Domnu?"

Tanaquil shook her head. "We can hardly guess ... mother of all sea-life; some vast half-animal half-vegetable thing rooted in the Abyss ... her tentacles embrace all deeps and shallows. And her cold mind has tentacles too, bitter and malevolent, to reach out into the minds of elukoi and morkani, through Caer Ys to the Hills, and mayhap even to Faerie itself ... you could never destroy her; she retreats into the dark gulfs and cannot be reached ..."

As in Orionë, a cold horror sickened Holly. She was glad then not to be near the sea.

"Things have not ended so ill as they might." Eilunieth had no anger in her. She awed Holly. "We are for the most part alive and well, and bound for Faerie. I mind that Mirror-mere is dry and broken, and those bright caverns dark now; but those we would be leaving anyway ... we are going home. Let that end all enmities. Soon these exiled years on Earth will be no more than the dream of a dream. It has passed. It has ended. Let it be forgot."

They came past the Great Hall for the last time. The world was heavy, white and golden. Holly zipped up her anorak. She missed a familiar face then, and wondered where Sandys was. Seeing the rest had turned aside, she followed them, meaning to ask.

Close to the wall of the Hall the snow was disturbed, and there was a newly-made mound and three single graves. In the fresh yellow-brown earth of the mound twenty or so spears were thrust, point upwards, and two banners were there also: on one a raven, on the other a stooping hawk.

Holly stopped without realising it. She knew the look of that fresh-turned earth. For her now it was not winter but early harvest-time, not snow-bright but sunlight; and there was a deep sickness inside her.

I was right, she thought, I was right. Anything's better than this. It's not many. But even one is too many.

She found Silverleaf at her side, sternly remote, and managed to ask, "Who are they?"

"Those who died last night, all in one tomb."

Holly counted the spears. Twenty-seven. "The two graves with hawk-banners?"

"Fiorin died last night. The other—Dalziel D'Ys, a Master Sorcerer."

The third grave had a white banner with a star on it. Silver, still without expression, said, "There is the last of the House of Diamond. There is Sandys."

"But he's a healer, not a fighter—"

"He is not either, being dead. I hate this place," she said, and still she would not cry. "He has been taken from me; and now must I hate you also, for you take my brother, too."

"Hold on," Holly protested, "it ain't me that's doing that. He don't even know I'm a girl, for Christ's sake."

Silver looked at her as if she spoke a foreign language. "I mean not you, but your world; all of you, out there."

She walked away, and Holly was left staring at the grave, eyes stinging; earth and snow suddenly blurred together. She thought, Sandys wanted Faerie as bad as any of them, and they've cheated him out of it, and he wasn't even armed.

She saw the elukoi were moving out. They had horse-drawn carts with hugely spoked wheels pulled up in a line through the city from the Hall to the river. Groups of elukoi and morkani with beasts stood arguing good-naturedly over this piece of furniture or that tapestry, or they rushed out with forgotten things that wouldn't fit on the carts anywhere, or poured hot wine for themselves while they stood back and watched the bustle. They had forgotten everything but their exodus, and Holly found herself drawn into their mood.

I'm alive, she thought, almost ashamed to be young and healthy and unhurt. Alive and glad of it.

She fell in with the others, walking beside Chris, and they went along the line of wagons towards its head.

21

The White City

The sun was only a hand's breadth over the horizon.

"It's early—we might get back without being copped."

"And if we don't?" Chris kicked moodily at the snow.

Holly assumed an innocent expression. "Well, I got up early to come over and see you . . ."

"And what did *I* do?"

". . . you got up early to come and see me! They won't get narky. It's too near Christmas."

"So it is . . . I won't be sorry to get back, neither."

"I will."

"Oh, you would! It's too goddamm exhausting for me, all this. Me for a nice quiet Christmas at home."

They passed through Brancaer, its houses empty and echoing now, the doors bare of their embroidered hangings. The snow-bound gardens were disturbed and bare. Holly noticed several carts loaded with young saplings, cuttings from trees, and sacks of seed. The elukoi were taking all they could.

But what about Fletch? Holly kept turning Silver's remarks over in her mind. She saw him then, but he was with Elathan.

Many greeted their party, saluting Oberon as King. Holly heard Eilunieth's name called, and the Harper's, and Tanaquil's. To her surprise there were many who called out to Chris; she was well known to the elukoi from the visits she had made to the Hills that autumn. Holly was not jealous. She preferred to be out of the limelight.

Fyraire was waiting at the head of the line to lead them, and he was brighter than the snow with the sun full on it. As they came up Hawkhunter sounded a long ringing call on his horn, and the whole cavalcade moved off at the speed of a slow walk towards the Gate. Holly, looking back, saw the long line of carts rutting the snow, the hill-dwellers and sea-people walking together, their pennants proud in the wind —the Hawk, the Rowan and the Raven. Early sunlight glittered on the windows of the deserted city.

The forest stood silent, leafless, smothered in snow. Branches bent under four times their own thickness of it; the east side of every tree-bole was plastered thick and foamy. Bare bark showed dark and wet. A pale sky was shining through stiff twigs.

Holly saw the Harper fall back to let Tanaquil talk privately with Oberon, that father and daughter so long sundered from each other. Then Westwind came up beside her and Chris with a flagon of pale golden wine. They drank. It was searingly cold, but it spread in Holly like fire.

She heard a harp strike up ahead in the knife-edge wind, and a song was taken up by many voices, but Mathurin Harper's over all:

"True Thomas lay on Huntlie bank
And a marvel he there did see:
A maid with flame-red hair unbound
Come riding by the Eildon Tree.

Her dress was of the grass-green silk,
Her mantle of the velvet fine;

> At every lock of her horse's mane
> Hung fifty silver bells and nine."

The wagons creaked and the hounds bayed and the silence of the woods was broken as they passed.

Holly, seeing a shadow out of the corner of her eye, found Fletcher by her side.

"That's a compliment to us," he said gravely. "The song is human, heard in elukoi halls in the high days that are gone: Thomas the Rhymer."

She saw Chris had gone off on her own, talking with elukoi whose names and faces she was unsure of: Starkweather, Greyeyes, Westwind.

"Fletcher—what are you going to do?"

> "True Thomas he pulled off his cap
> And bowed him low down on his knee:
> 'Hail to thee, Mary, Queen of Heaven!
> For thy peer on earth could never be.'

> 'O no, O no; True Thomas mine,
> That name does not belong to me.
> I am the Queen of fair Elfland
> And came full far to visit thee.' "

"How d'you mean 'do'?"

"Don't give me that. I been talking to Silver. She says you're not going with them. Why not?"

"It's no choice. Elathan's explained that. There's no way a human could live in Faerie, not now, not even one brought up in the Hills like me."

She saw he was empty-handed, bringing nothing of his former life out of the Hills with him. They walked silent under the great beeches. The snow was pocked with animal tracks, fox and badger and others less recognisable.

" 'Harp and sing, Thomas,' she said,
 'Come with me to my own country.
 I'll give to you a harp of gold,
 A silken cloak, and kisses three.'

 'To me the priest would bar the church
 If I hazard my soul with thee—
 I'll not come for harp and cloak
 But I'll come for your kisses three.' "

"I didn't know what you'd want to do—I didn't know you wouldn't have a choice."

"Nor did I—Holly, it wouldn't be so bad if I did. I want to stay. And I want to go, because I think, how can I leave him?"

You'll be better off when you have, boy. Holly still didn't like Elathan at all. "It's final, then."

"It's final."

"She's mounted on her milk-white steed,
 She's taken True Thomas up behind;
 The silver bells at the bridle ring,
 The steed runs faster than the wind."

"I'm sorry about what I said in the Park."

"Oh hell—me too," Holly admitted, "I've got a lousy temper sometimes. And it wasn't true."

"Nor what I said; I know that now."

"So—forget it, right?" And she felt warm.

" 'O see that road so hard to pass,
So narrow it is and so straight?
You'll find on that no priest or friar
For it leads to Heaven's gate.

'And see that other, easy, road
So broad and free from mire?
Though fair with flowers be the start
Its end is in Hell's fire.

'But see the path that winds away
By bracken and by white birch tree?
A pleasant road to fair Elfland,
This night thou'lt be there with me.' "

It hadn't occurred to Holly before. "Fletch—how are they
going to get there?"
"The Gate, he said, "the Gate, and the Lord of Stars."

"O they rode on and further on
And they waded rivers above the knee;
And they saw neither sun nor moon
But they heard the roaring of the sea.

He has gotten a cloak and a golden harp,
And kisses three from the elven Queen;
But seven hundred years were gone and past
Till Thomas ever on earth was seen."

They came to the Gate and Hawkhunter blew the halt.
Holly saw Chris go forward to say goodbye, but she hung
back. An idea had come to her.
Fletcher went again to Elathan, and the man who had

been his father embraced and kissed him, and they did not speak. Silver moved to take the old man's arm.

Go through the Gate swiftly—Fyraire's contact came to all three, Holly, Chris and Fletcher—*for I must make it take me to my own place; and from there to Faerie is a short step.*

She did not move when Chris and Fletcher went to the Gate; she was talking urgently to Fyraire.

"You said there was an overlap, didn't you? Between here and there. So if being spell-breakers and humans means we can't come with you, surely we could at least see it?"

"Who wants to?" Chris interrupted. "I seen enough. Let's get home."

Fletcher said, "I've made my choice. I don't want to see what I can't have."

The boy is closest to the truth. It is not good to see that which cannot be had for all the gold or love in the world, and know that it cannot be had.

"You two carry on—I'll be with you in a bit." She watched them go. They think I'm crazy. Maybe I am. But I'll see it through to the end. All of it.

Do not say no warning was given—the range widened to include the rest—*now, follow me.*

He passed through the Gate, and after him Oberon, Elathan and Eilunieth in a group; then Holly and the Harper and Tanaquil; then the other elukoi and morkani. At the Gate Holly put her hand over her eyes and carried on walking, holding Mathurin's arm.

It was worse than before, much worse. Before it had made her dizzy and sick, but this was like a blow in the stomach. She stumbled, breathless and sweating, the glow of the wine shaken out of her; stone cold sober.

"My own place" the Unicorn had said. Holly recognised

it. Silver birches were leafless still, buds not broken, the dips
and hollows filled with red bracken; leaves underfoot, yellow
and brown; the sky an incredibly wide expanse of blue; the
sun too high for winter.

I saw this at Highrock—Holly let go of the Harper's arm
—at midsummer. Clear as I see it now.

A rutted track twisted among the trees, easy going for
the wagons. Holly pushed ahead and found herself by Fyraire
and the King.

Oberon said, "How long is it that we have been gone
from our own land?"

*A year and a day. All the thousands of years that have passed
over you have only sufficed there to turn summer to winter, and
winter again to summer.*

"And where shall we return, Lord?"

To the place where you left it, you and all your people.

They topped a rise and the trees ended. Holly, still walking
forward, found her way barred by the Unicorn.

You may look only. It was a warning. *Stand here by me.
Oberon's people! There is your home. Go to it while the way
is open.*

"This wood borders on Faerie?"

The Silver Wood borders on most places.

The line of wagons rumbled ahead and out of the wood,
and with them went the elukoi, the morkani, and the beasts.
Holly watched them go. For a few yards there was grass,
then it petered out and sandy soil showed through, and that
in turn gave way to hard flat sand. She saw that, then she
was distracted by Oberon.

He had gone forward first, now he stood alone on the
sand. She saw him take a deep breath and straighten up, and
it was more than that—his whole body grew and straightened
skyward. It took him as a fire takes paper, the colour flooded

back into his skin and the wrinkles went out of his face; his golden eyes cleared, and his hair flamed and reddened like a sunrise.

Tall he was, and strong and fair and wise; Oberon, Lord of Faerie.

Others followed: Eilunieth, Elathan, Mathurin, Tanaquil, Seahawk, Brionis and Silver—the age and the cares of Earth went from them like a bad dream. It was not that they became young. They became ageless.

And Holly was alone. Those who glanced carelessly back and saw her had no recognition in their eyes, not even Elathan; not even Mathurin. She knew then why Elathan would not have taken Fletcher with him even if he could. They had passed from a nightmare into the waking world.

Fyraire stirred. *Look well. If you must look, then look well.*

Holly looked away and beyond the people of Faerie.

It was summer and early morning, she felt the heat of it on her face. She stood on the verge of a wide sandy beach, with the waves beating far ahead as the tide went out.

A long rocky spit of land reached out into the sea and ended at a craggy mount. On this was a city, white and gold in the sunrise, hazed in flying spray.

Holly forgot the elukoi and morkani then. She knew that city. It was impossible, but she knew it. And she wanted it desperately.

Plain white stone houses with their roofs of enamelled blue tiles, bright as kingfishers; glinting here and there with gold—she knew them. The terraced streets that criss-crossed up the hill, the arches and bridges and gardens with their fountains, the courtyards with shivering lime trees; she knew them all. She could have named the shops and warehouses and the docks, and the cobbled streets that led down to the harbour. It was all white light and gold, and blue shadows rich in sea-haze.

She thought it must be somewhere she had dreamed of, or seen as a child; not knowing how familiar that perilous Kingdom can seem.

A strong wind out of the east whipped the sea to foam, and brought her the clean smell of salt; and fish-smells too from the market at the mount's base, where fishing boats were drawn up on the shingle. In the waterside docks were high-prowed sailing ships with canvas bellying deep in the wind as they strained to set sail.

I know that place, she thought or said or sang. *Every street, every cliff above town. I know the ships in port and their captains, I know what fabled lands they set sail for. Oberon, I know it as well as you do. This is home—*

Unknowingly she stepped forward, and the Unicorn lowered his head and a horn barred her way.

You have seen. Go back. That would kill you.

"I don't care. I'm going there."

Get back!

She made a dive past him, but he was there before her. The horn stabbed at her throat and she dodged, leaped back again to avoid the flailing hooves, and slipped.

"No!"

He was a white fury. She scrambled up and ran, pushing through the bracken. Hooves crashed behind her, she felt his hot breath, and she ran; headed away from that white city.

He's going to kill me! She slipped again, cannoned off a birch tree and ran on, scarcely breaking stride. The ground dipped; opened into a trickle of a stream. She hurdled it, heard him scatter stones close on her heels.

"I won't go there—I won't!"

Her foot caught in a pothole. She fell and twisted sideways. The white horn struck within an inch of her and split a birch trunk as thick as her leg. Holly was up and away, one shoe left behind in the mud, as the Unicorn wrenched free from the pale wood. She ran, limping.

Ahead, the trees were clearing—it would give her room to run—she sprinted out of the wood and over the snowy grass, skidded across a slushy road and fetched up hard against a low brick wall.

No noise except her own sobbing, heaving breath.

Holly opened her eyes, clinging to the wall as if it were a lifebelt, feeling as if her chest had been scoured out from the inside. She was looking down at railway lines. Not a wall —the parapet of the bridge; Hallows Hill.

She looked over her shoulder—an ordinary road and a hill and, in the distance, Birchdale Junction. Dazed, she bent down to feel her wet shoeless foot and test the ankle. He was right, she thought. The SilverWood borders on most places. I've seen the last of that shoe anyway.

In the white expanse of the marshes were two dots of colour. She waved both arms over her head and waited until Fletcher and Chris waved back, then took the path across the mud.

It was for assurance she looked for the Downs. They were unforested. She could see everything between her and those ancient hills clearly; the contours of the land under the snow, the houses of Combe Marsh and of Deepdean under Chalk Head, and every dip and fold and snow-filled hollow of the Downs themselves. Frosty air struck her newly cold. A gull curved high on the wind and cried. Her shadow went tall into the west. It was good; but not good enough. She squeezed her eyes shut but the hot tears ran down her cheeks.

I had to look. She wiped her face. I had to look, didn't

I. What was the name of that city? I knew it—I knew all about it—but it's gone now. What did he say? That which cannot be had for all the gold or love in the world. And still to want it.

"We thought we'd lost you for good," Chris grunted, short of breath from the slope up to the bridge. "Well—what did you see?"

"You didn't miss anything." She smiled and lied. "I didn't get there—I don't think *we* can. And I lost a shoe somewhere!"

"Oh, Jesus, girl!" Chris saw her one wet sock and shouted with laughter. "Trust you. It could only happen to you!"

"Oh ha ha. Very funny. How am I supposed to get home —hop?"

Fletcher pointed down the road. "You've got the devil's luck. There's the early bus."

"Good. I'm starved, just plain *starved*. Me for bacon and eggs. And beans and toast and fried spud—"

Holly realised it had been fourteen hours since she'd eaten. "Oh, don't!"

Fletcher took one last look back at the Hills. "We seem to have come out of this pretty well, wouldn't you say? They are OK, and so are we."

"I should think so! Since we managed most of it between us three—right Holly?"

"Hmm?" Us all right? she thought. Two weeks and we're back in that buggerly school with bitch-Gabriel, and she's going to try and beat hell out of me. And there's exams. And my goddamm parents. It's too much. And never to see the city again . . .

But already her fingers itched for paints to trace its shape on paper, and Chris was waiting; so she scraped up a grin and said, "Right on!"

Fletcher held up a hand. "Listen."

Someone in one of the nearby houses had a radio on, and the old carol came out thinly over the snow. The three of them listened; and laughed; and flagged down the bus. The carol played on in the deserted morning:

> "The holly and the ivy,
> When they are both full grown;
> Of all the trees that are in the wood
> The holly bears the crown.
> O the rising of the sun
> And the running of the deer,
> The playing of the merry organ:
> Sweet singing in the choir . . ."